CONFLICT OF INTEREST

CONFLICT OF INTEREST

Aileen Armitage

Severn House Large Print
London & New York

This first large print edition published in Great Britain 2006 by
SEVERN HOUSE LARGE PRINT BOOKS LTD of
9-15 High Street, Sutton, Surrey, SM1 1DF.
This title first published in Great Britain 2005 by
Severn House Publishers, London and New York.
This first large print edition published in the USA 2006 by
SEVERN HOUSE PUBLISHERS INC., of
595 Madison Avenue, New York, NY 10022.

British Library Cataloguing in Publication Data

Armitage, Aileen, 1930 -
    Conflict of interest. - Large print ed.
    1.   Woollen and worsted manufacture - England - Huddersfield -
         Fiction
    2.   Great Britain - History - 1789-1820 - Fiction
    3.   Historical fiction
    4.   Large type books
    I.   Title II. Lindley, Erica.   Shadow of Dungeon Wood
    823.9'14 [F]

    ISBN-10: 0-7278-7493-4

Printed and bound in Great Britain by
MPG Books Ltd, Bodmin, Cornwall.

For my father, ERIC ARMITAGE,
whose deep love of Yorkshire and its history
he passed on to me, inspiring me to write
this book.

AUTHOR'S NOTE

This story is basically true. All the events described in the book actually occurred in or near Huddersfield during the year 1812, with the exception of Atkinson's mill fire which actually took place in Colne Bridge in February 1818. For the sake of unity, however, I have telescoped this incident to happen nearer Longroyd Bridge in 1812.

Most of the characters and all of the place names are those of real people and places. Mellors, Thorpe and Booth were all protagonists in the Luddite cause, and Radcliffe the magistrate who sought to bring them to justice. Josiah Denshaw in my story is loosely based on William Horsfall, owner of Ottiwells Mill at Marsden, who was murdered by the Luddites.

Only Jess Drake and his family spring from my imagination, but they must be typical of hundreds of Colne Valley families who suffered such distress at the time of the Industrial Revolution.

One

The wind howled about the little stone cottage, shaking the small panes of glass in the windows and clattering the door in its shrunken frame. But the rise and fall of the wind's sobbing rage could not blot out the agonised screams of a woman struggling in childbirth.

Jess Drake sat stiffly in his chair by the empty grate feeling the nape of his neck tense with anxiety as he heard his wife's cries, and the fingers of his little daughter digging into his knees. Opposite him Jenny sat sewing with earnest concentration. Abigail's wide eyes gazed up at him in alarm, and she began to whimper.

'Now come on, lass, there's no cause for thee to weep,' Jess murmured, stroking her soft hair and thinking how big and clumsy his work-roughened hand looked on her fair head. But inwardly he did not feel so sure. Maggie had never had an easy time of it before, and she'd been on with this one for

9

the Lord knew how many hours already. He'd have gone in to her before now, but Mrs Bates would never allow it. Bless her, she was a game one was Maggie. Three daughters she'd borne him, and each birth more dangerous than the last but she'd set her heart on giving him the son he craved. Twice she'd succeeded but one little creature was too frail for this world after his lengthy efforts to arrive in it, and he'd gasped but a few breaths before leaving it again, and then young Jess had struggled through five years before being crushed at the mill gate by a laden cart.

Maggie had set her lips and determined she'd give him another son yet. That was typical of her. She was a game one right enough, and Jess thanked his lucky stars for giving him such a wife. Never a one to complain was Maggie, no matter what blows befell them. Not even when their peaceful life in the cottage, spinning and weaving the fine Yorkshire wool had had to cease, and Jess had been forced to go and work in the mill.

The door to the other room opened, and a woman appeared. Jess started. Not till that moment had he realised that Maggie's cries no longer competed with the howling wind outside.

The woman stood, feet astride, in the doorway.

'Well, Jess Drake, she's done it.'

Jess gazed at the nurse, uncomprehendingly.

'Jess, your Maggie's done it. She's given thee a son. Go down on thy knees and thank God for His mercy, for she's alive and so is t' bairn.'

Jess rose and crossed the flagstoned floor of the little room in two strides and made to pass the nurse, but she took hold of his sleeve. 'No, not yet, Jess. She's worn out from so long a labour and ready for sleep. I'll bring thy son to thee.' She turned and re-entered the little room, reappearing with a small bundle of sheeting. 'See,' she said, pulling back a corner for him to see. The girls crowded in, anxious to see too, and Jess could just glimpse a tiny, red crumpled face, the eyes closed and a finger in its mouth.

'Is he alive?' he asked.

'Oh aye, don't fash thissen. Did tha not hear him cry?'

Jess shook his head. It was enough that he had a son and he was alive and well. The nurse, having allowed the girls to peep and wonder, bustled back to her patient. Jess felt now he could breathe again, and longed to fill his lungs with fresh moorland air.

'I'm off out,' he announced to Jenny. 'Get Abigail off to bed now and tell Mrs Bates I'll not be long.'

His long legs carried him swiftly across the moor. The wind was lessening now and far below in the valley he could see the lights of Huddersfield winking between the trees. Unthinkingly his feet directed him to the little inn on the edge of the moor and he strode in, welcoming the blast of warmth that greeted him, murmured a few words to the landlord and sat on a settle in the corner. Looking around him he could see none of his acquaintances to whom he could break his good news, so he sat back and quaffed his ale contentedly, hugging his pleasure to him. At last he had fathered another healthy son whom he could cherish just as he had Maria and Jenny and Abigail, and who would grow up to follow in his footsteps.

Jess's thoughts faltered. What footsteps? Once Jess had been a craftsman weaver with his own loom taking up the whole of the upstairs room of his cottage, and he had taken great pride in the fine lengths of wool he had made and carried weekly to the Cloth Hall in Huddersfield to sell. But no more. Mills had replaced private looms and mill-owners wanted, not craftsmen, but merely men to tend their machines, machines which churned out cloth by the yard faster than a dozen handloom weavers could have woven it.

Weavers stubborn enough to try to carry on working in their homes had soon found out how impossible it was to fight these men with money and machines. One by one they had given up the struggle and slunk off, Jess amongst them, to work in the mill, where at least money enough to feed a family could be earned.

So of what use to his son was that loom upstairs, rotting and idle, Jess sighed. What heritage, what family pride had he to hand on to his much-wanted son? It was a hard world and no mistake, that robbed a man of all the pride he had.

Jess's musing was suddenly broken by the fierce crash of a man's fist on the table under the lamplight. A group of men were listening attentively to the dark young man who was speaking in a low, earnest voice. The emptied ale-glasses clattered together under the sharpness of his fist blow on the oak table.

'Hirst and Balderstone have had a taste of it and by God, I swear old Denshaw shall have his taste of it yet,' the young man vowed, 'or my name's not George Mellors!'

There was such an air of venom and determination in his low voice that Jess looked up from his tankard curiously. A pallid youth on the far side of the table, facing Jess, hissed something quietly under his breath and nodded slightly in Jess's direction. Instantly the eyes of all the men turned towards Jess, who coloured with embarrassment at being caught thus eavesdropping, and he looked back at his tankard again, watching the froth draining down the inside.

The silence was menacing. Jess swilled the last dregs of ale about in the bottom of the tankard and upended it to his lips. Thus he was able to see over the rim the five curious faces watching him. The dark youth snapped his fingers suddenly, bringing the silence to an end.

'I know thee – live up on t' moor, beyond t' wood. Weaver, aren't tha?'

Jess set his tankard down and nodded. 'Aye,' then as an afterthought he added, 'Leastways, I was.'

The youth turned back to his companions with a smile. 'See lads? He's one of us, so there's no need to fret.' He rose and strode across to Jess's corner, his hand outstretched. 'George Mellors, craftsman cropper by trade like my mates here.'

Jess saw the horny callous on his extended wrist and knew he was speaking the truth for the hoof was the life-long mark of all croppers, caused by the handle of the long shears they used to crop the pile on the lengths of wool. 'Jess Drake,' he said, clasping the other man's hand firmly.

Mellors' eyes lit up in recognition. 'Drake? Oh aye, thy family's been weavers hereabouts for many a year. Had to give it up and go in t' mill, hasta?'

'Aye.'

'Whose mill?'

'Denshaw's, Longroyd Bridge.'

Jess saw Mellors look sharply across to his companions and then back to Jess. 'Don't sit supping alone, lad – come and join us at table. Landlord, more ale!'

Mellors took Jess's arm and drew him across to the centre table. The other men shuffled their chairs to make room to admit him to the circle and the beer glasses were refilled. Mellors turned amiably to Jess.

'Had any trouble down at thy place?' he asked.

'Trouble? Why, no. What kind of trouble?' Jess asked in surprise. 'Denshaw's isn't a bad place, they tell me, as mills go.'

The pallid youth, dark-browed and sullen-looking, spoke at last. 'Nobody broke up t' machines yet then?'

Jess saw Mellors' warning frown directed towards the youth. 'Why no,' he said, 'though I have heard as some mills 'ave 'ad trouble that way.'

'And more will yet, I've no doubt,' said Mellors.

'Oh, not here, surely,' protested Jess. 'Nottingham has, I know, wi' t' stocking workers, but never here in t' Colne Valley.'

'Why not?' asked Mellors. 'Principle's t' same, isn't it? Machines are robbing t' craftsman of his trade here just as there. Tha should know, Jess lad, tha's suffered.'

Indeed, thought Jess sadly as he tossed back his ale. From the fourteen shillings a week he'd reckoned to earn five years ago he'd dropped to less than six shillings working on his own loom, far too little to feed his family on. It had been then that he and Maggie had had to make the agonising decision to give up the hopeless struggle, lower his pride and work in the mill. And even the ten shillings he brought home weekly now from Denshaw's was far from sufficient to keep the pangs of hunger from his children's stomachs. But for Maria's six shillings they'd have starved altogether.

'And it'll be our turn next,' muttered the dark, sullen youth.

'Aye, tha'rt right there, Ben lad,' said Mellors. 'Wi' all these new cropping frames I hear talk of being brought into t' mills, there'll be no work for us in t' cropping shops.'

'Tha'rt all in t' same cropping shop then?' Jess asked.

'At my stepfather's shop at Longroyd Bridge,' Mellors replied.

'John Wood's?'

'Aye, that's right.'

'All t' wool from Denshaw's goes there for cropping.'

'Not for much longer though. I hear as Denshaw is getting cropping frames into t' factory soon.'

'Is he then?' Jess mused. 'I haven't heard.'

'Unless someone stops him first,' observed the youth called Ben with a smirk.

'And I think there's some as'll try,' murmured a sandy-haired young man who had not spoken till now.

'No doubt, Bill. Them Luddites is spreading all over t' place,' commented Mellors.

'Luddites – that's it,' murmured Jess. 'That's what they called them machine-breakers in Nottingham.'

'And not only there,' Mellors corrected him. 'They've slashed machine-made bolts of cloth i' Leeds and attacked and burnt a mill i' Wakefield. They're getting nearer.'

Jess savoured the news in wonder. 'And have none of them been caught? ·Surely someone recognised who they were?'

'Not they,' Mellors exclaimed. 'They were all either disguised or had their faces blackened. And they're well trained at striking quickly and escaping into t' night.'

'But all that damage – where's it leading them?' Jess enquired. 'What good's it doing them?'

'Tell him, Ben Walker,' Mellors said patiently and sat back. Ben took a draught of ale and smiled across at Jess.

'Well, it's clear as day, isn't it? If all machines to do t' weaving and t' cropping are smashed to smithereens, the only ones as can do t' work then are t' craftsmen, t' handloom weavers and handcroppers. It gives us our jobs back, don't it, thine and ours?'

'I suppose so.' Jess's mind ticked over slowly for it always took him time to ponder over a new idea.

'Bill Thorpe here, and Will Hall and Tom Smith, they're handcroppers like Mellors and me,' said Walker, 'and they're not anxious to lose their work to a machine any more than thee. They've got families to feed. Dost honestly blame a man for

18

wanting to go on working at t' trade he's become a master at? Cansta blame him for trying to stop machines coming?'

Mellors signalled Walker to stop. 'He's right tha knows, Jess lad,' he sighed. 'A man must do what he must, whether he likes it or not.'

'Reckon tha'rt right,' Jess murmured.

'Hasta family?' Mellors enquired.

'Aye, three lasses – and a lad born just tonight,' Jess answered with a tinge of pride.

'Well now, that calls for a toast. Landlord!' Mellors cried. The innkeeper hastened to refill the tankards and Mellors raised his to Jess. 'To thy lad, and may he be as fine a weaver as his father,' he said.

'To thy lad,' the others assented, and they all drank. Jess felt proud. Pleasant fellows these, all respectable earnest men with a trade to their fingers. He was proud both of their acclaim and of his newly-restored status as father of a son. Tonight the world was fine and he drank deeply, knowing it would seem as chill and cheerless as before in the morning. But for tonight he felt a man again.

Mellors clapped him jovially on the shoulder. 'I'm right glad we've met, Jess Drake,' he said, 'and I hope we shall see thee again soon.'

'No doubt,' Jess answered, hoping they would.

'Tha'rt a good fellow wi' a bit o' gumption in that head o' thine,' said Mellors. 'We'd be proud to 'ave thee in our company.'

Jess's heart swelled. 'Thankee, I'd be honoured. But I mun be getting back 'ome now. Tomorrow night?'

'Tomorrow it shall be, lad.'

The other men joined Mellors in bidding Jess goodnight and he picked up his cap and went out. Outside, away from the lamplight, the night was dark and the wind blowing still, helping to clear the muzziness out of Jess's brain. It had been a pleasant evening in the inn and he looked forward to meeting the amiable young Mellors and his friends again. Men with brains they were, able to think of positive action to better their lot instead of just suffering it like most folk. This Luddite business, for instance. Not that Jess approved of destruction for its own sake, but to protect a man and his family, that was a different matter. If a man didn't stand up for himself along with his mates, then who would? Perhaps he could talk it over with Maggie, for she was a sensible lass and he never did aught without her approval. Not yet though – in a day or two perhaps, when she was feeling better.

On his homeward journey up the hill towards his cottage Jess skirted the fringe of Dungeon Wood. He rarely went directly through it at night for the Lord knew, even the open moors held dangers enough by night for a man, whether afoot or on horseback, but crossing a dark wood was courting trouble. Yet the place held a strange attraction for him, for it was here on summer evenings that he had first courted Maggie, away from the prying eyes of the local people who knew them both well.

'Tha'rt not afraid in t' wood wi' me, art tha, lass?' he'd said to her, and her only answer had been to cradle closer in his arms, a warm, soft little body she'd been then, with eyes wide and trusting like the rabbits he snared. She spoke little then, as now, but he'd known that she loved him and would always love him.

But much had changed since then, not least Maggie herself, still quiet enough it was true, and faithful and patient as any man could wish, but where was the rosy warm armful now? Bearing children and scraping to feed them on a pittance had changed his loving lass to a grey, faded woman with lines where the smiles had once been. She looked old already, although not yet thirty-six. The welcoming arms had given way to cold refusal and a bony back turned on him in bed more often than not. Not that she didn't still care for him, of that he was certain, but the threat of more mouths to feed had been a constant worry to her. But for her determination to provide him with another son, Jess would have found no comfort in a cold world.

But now that son had arrived, would Maggie turn her back on him again? Jess pushed the unwelcome thought from his mind and strode home across the moor whistling, though the sound was lost to his ears in the wind.

He lifted the sneck of the cottage door and tiptoed in so as not to disturb either Maggie or the sleeping children. To his surprise Jenny lay curled up asleep alongside Maggie in their big bed.

'Maggie, art awake, lass?' he whispered.

'Aye,' a buried voice came from under the bedclothes.

'Jenny's in my place.'

'Aye, she were hungry and cold. I told her to get in by me,' Maggie's voice came back in the darkness. 'Get thee upstairs, Jess, and sleep wi' Abigail.'

Jess turned and tiptoed out of the room without answering. He was bewildered at being turned out of his bed for the first time in all their married life. He felt hurt and lost.

Maria's dark, tousled head lay on the moonlit pillow on the far side of the upstairs room. So she was home at last. As he crawled in with Abigail's small, warm body Jess reflected that maybe Maggie hadn't meant it deliberately as a sign of rejecting him. Maybe it was only as she said, and Jenny was cold. Maybe when Maggie had recovered from the baby's birth ... He glowed again as he thought of the baby, his son.

Abigail turned over and whimpered. 'What's the matter, lass?'

The little body huddled up to him. 'I'm hungry,' a small voice said in the dark.

Jess was hungry too. They all were. Thin gruel for an evening meal was not enough for a man after a day's work, nor even for a little lass like Abigail. Jess crept downstairs again and returned with a piece of oatcake in his hand.

'Here, lass, eat this and don't leave any telltale crumbs in t' bed,' he admonished the child, and the little one leapt up and grabbed it from him, swallowing it in eager mouthfuls. Jess lay down again beside her, trying to ignore the pangs in his own belly, and turned over in his mind how to explain the absence of the oatcake in the morning.

Two

The first faint grey shafts of dawn were streaking the eastern horizon as Jess and Maria set off to walk down the hill to work. Jess strode out comfortably enough in his old boots but felt guilty that Maria with her bare feet had to leap from grass mound to heather hillock to avoid the filthy stones of the road. Still, it wasn't as cruel for her as it had been when the snow lay deep on the moor.

'Some day I'll get thee some shoes, lass,' he promised, but he knew it was a faint-hearted vow. Where could he ever find money for shoes when there was little enough to be had for food? His own boots were the kind offering of his cousin Kate whose husband had been killed in the coal-mine. But for Kate he'd have suffered the agony of chilblains and frostbite as others did.

'I'll get some for mesen,' Maria's reply came in the semi-darkness, proud and resentful. 'I'll not always be barefoot.'

24

She was a Drake right enough, thought Jess. Proud and determined, just like all the valley folk. She'd always been more determined than most, right from being a babe. Self-willed and stubborn, Maggie had said, after coping with Maria's childish demands and whims all day, but Jess thought Maggie was being unjust to the child. He'd never quite understood Maria himself. She was different from his other children. Even in appearance, being so dark-haired and dark-eyed where Maggie and himself and all their other children had been fair. And by nature too she was different. Quiet on the whole and strong, but with occasional outbursts of temper that frightened him.

These days, however, she was less temperamental than she used to be. Growing up, he supposed. He looked at her thoughtfully in the half light as she picked her way carefully beside him. Yes, she was indeed grown up. At eighteen she was a woman in full flower with the rounded fullness he remembered in Maggie in days gone by. It was surprising really that Maria could be so firm and rosy when his other children remained so pale and thin. Still, perhaps it was to be expected in Jenny, with that bad cough of hers.

His thoughts returned to the shoes. Maria seemed so certain she could procure some for herself. He wondered idly if she had any plan in mind. Quick-witted, was Maria, of that there was no doubt. That was another way in which she was different from himself and Maggie and the others. Quick to understand, quick in answer and at one time always quick to anger. Had she in fact worked out some way to obtain those shoes? The only way he could think of her getting them, money being so short, was if she was to go up to one of the big houses and beg – but surely she'd never do that? Not Maria, with her pride and dignity and all?

Denshaw's mill loomed into sight. In a minute he'd have lost her inside the mill. Tentatively he turned to her.

'Maria, love,' he said hesitantly, 'about them shoes. Tha doesn't plan to do aught stupid like, dost tha?' He did not really understand what fears flitted through his brain, only that he feared for her. And however strange and incomprehensible she was to him, she was one of his own.

Maria stared at him for a moment. Then she pursed her lips. 'Tha doesn't need to fret thissen over me, father,' she said coolly. 'I can fend for meself.' Then she turned away and went ahead of him into the mill.

The church clock struck five.

Jess sighed and shook his head, then followed Maria in.

Up at Brackenhurst, the large, rambling house on the hill, Josiah Denshaw sat down to breakfast opposite his son. In answer to his offhand 'Good morning, Father,' the old man simply grunted and reached for the newspaper beside his plate.

'Hullo,' he said in irritation, 'what's this? My *Leeds Mercury* is all rumpled and creased. Now look here, Robert, tha knows I don't like anyone to touch my paper before I've read it, I've told thee oft enough.'

'Indeed you have, Papa, and equally often I've assured you that I'm not to blame. I'm not remotely interested in the price of grain per ton, nor in Wellington's goings-on in the war. You must look for some other culprit.' Robert Denshaw pushed his chair back from the table, flicked some crumbs from his elegant lace cravat and rose languidly.

Old Denshaw snorted. 'Then it must be Sukey. Where is t' lass, hasta seen her?'

Robert shrugged and went to gaze out of the window. 'I rather think she's gone down to the kitchen to order some dish for dinner tonight.'

The door opened and a handsome, dark-eyed girl swept in. 'Ah, Papa!' she said,

bending over him and placing an affection-
ate peck on his forehead. Denshaw eyed her
severely and pointed dramatically to his
newspaper.

'Was it thee, Sukey, as rumpled my *Mer-cury*?'

'Susannah, Papa, not Sukey, and yes I did.
I wanted to keep *au fait* with what is happening.'

'Keep what?'

'She means keep abreast of current affairs,
Father,' explained Robert, turning from the
window. 'Though why, I cannot imagine. I
find it all too boring for words.'

'Tha wouldn't think so if tha 'ad to earn t'
brass as I do,' retorted Denshaw angrily. 'I
'ave to watch t' price of wool 'cause that's
where thy bread comes from, lad. And all t'
rest of the trimmings tha's used to, thee and
Sukey, gallivanting off to London and all.
Tha can spend brass wi' out difficulty, the
pair on thee, by thump tha can.'

Robert slumped in an armchair and
started to clean his nails with a silver tooth-
pick. His obvious inattention riled the old
man.

'Tha's had the fruit of all my labours, thee
and Sukey – good schooling, fine clothes
and all. Thy mother didn't live long enough
to enjoy t' brass, but the two of thee have

had all money can buy.'

'And you're proud of us,' Susannah reminded him, reaching for the toast. 'You know you are, Papa.'

'Indeed I am, lass. 'Appen if I'd been able to speak genteel like thee I'd a put up for Parliament. As it is, I'm content to stay a millowner and watch thee and Robert and thy fine friends doing well. And one day, mayhap, Robert will take over t' mill...'

Robert sprang from his chair. 'Not for many a long day, I hope, Father. You can manage it so much better than I.'

'Just so long as tha gets brass to keep thee in thy fine ways, I know,' murmured his father. 'But I'll not always be here. It wouldn't 'arm for thee to come down to t' mill now and again and see how things shape there.'

Robert sighed audibly. Susannah interrupted before her father could take umbrage again. 'I should like above all things to inspect the mill, Papa. May I?'

Her air of eager interest surprised old Denshaw. He eyed his daughter curiously. 'Well, it's not usual for a lass to concern herself wi' business,' he said slowly and thoughtfully, 'but it might not be a bad idea for one of thee to know what goes on.'

'I was reading in the *Leeds Mercury* about

the unrest among mill workers, you see,' Susannah explained, 'about the hardships they claim they suffer, the low wages and poor conditions.'

Denshaw's face reddened with anger. 'Not i' my mill!' he exclaimed sharply. 'I pay fair rates and there's no hardship i' my mill! If I'd known that's the kind of fancy idea tha gets i' thy head from thy fine boarding school, I should never a sent thee there!'

Susannah smiled and patted his arm. 'It wasn't school, Papa. They only taught us to walk and speak nicely, to speak a little French and how to order a meal and set a table elegantly.'

'That's all a woman needs to know,' Denshaw grunted.

'But I want to know what's happening elsewhere too,' Susannah exclaimed. 'How the war against Napoleon is going, why General Vyse has sent the King's Bays into Huddersfield – that's why I was reading your *Mercury*.'

'Thee just leave my paper alone. It's not a woman's place to concern herself wi' business and politics – that's men's affairs. I just wish thy brother would do a bit.'

'But how else will I understand what is happening, Papa?'

Denshaw put his fork down and considered while he chewed. 'If there's aught tha doesn't understand about politics, just ask me, lass, and I'll explain in a way tha can follow easily. But leave my *Mercury* alone.'

'And can I go with you to the mill Papa – please?'

Denshaw sat back to consider, eyeing his daughter thoughtfully. 'Aye,' he said at last. 'It wouldn't do any 'arm for t' workers to see what fine folks the Denshaws are. Tha'll be a credit to me. And what about thee, Robert? Wilt tha come too?'

'Oh Papa!' Robert's voice registered pained boredom. 'It's such a vile, dirty place. I'd rather not. Take Sukey if she's so minded and she'll tell me all about it, I've no doubt.'

'Susannah, if you please,' said his sister, and left the room.

The uncertain morning had resolved itself into a fine, fresh spring day by the time Josiah Denshaw ordered the carriage to take himself and Susannah down to the mill. Robert still declined to come, much to the old man's annoyance, but Sukey helped to atone for his son's indifference by her keen interest and lively questioning.

'Why is that little child sitting there?' she asked as soon as they arrived at the mill, pointing to the grey-faced mite sitting in the

31

niche in the wall alongside the huge gates.

'It's his job to open and shut t' gates for t' wagons,' Denshaw explained. 'He's too small yet for heavier work.'

Susannah's eyes widened. 'It seems to me those huge gates are heavy enough for a man, let alone a child,' she commented.

Denshaw strode inside, nodding recognition to the workers who paused in their work only long enough to doff their caps to him. Susannah hurried after him.

'Heavens, isn't it noisy in here,' she exclaimed, clapping her hands to her ears. Denshaw made no answer. To him the relentless roar of the machines spelt trade and success and he loved the sound. The only occasions on which they lay idle, as on Sundays and when the summer droughts dried up the Colne and no longer did his water wheel spin, were melancholy days indeed. Some day Susannah, and Robert too for that matter would come to realise that the sound of machines meant money. Or brass, he called it, but Susannah and Robert with their refined way of speaking would call it money. And when they did realise it, they'd appreciate the sound too.

'And so dirty too!' Susannah was still exclaiming with surprise at the state of the factory.

'There's an old Yorkshire saying, lass, where there's muck there's brass,' Denshaw told her.

Susannah lifted the hem of her skirt clear of the filthy floor and stepped disdainfully into the main room, where the weaving was in progress. Here the clamour of machines was so deafening that only by shouting could conversation take place, and even then it was done more by lip-reading than by sound. It amused old Denshaw to watch Susannah's eyes widen even further to see all this whirring, clanking mass of machinery, with small children darting hither and thither between the close-packed rows of machines, and the overlookers parading watchfully up and down, clutching their leather straps. A tall, lean man with a mop of fair hair pulled off his cap and nodded to them.

'Morning, Drake,' Denshaw shouted. 'Where's Briggs?' Denshaw saw Drake's gaze flutter the length of the room and back, searching for the head overlooker.

'Don't know, Master Denshaw. He were here a minute gone.'

'When tha see him, tell him I'm waiting in t' office.'

'Aye, sir.'

Denshaw drew Susannah into the grimy

little office where she drew a deep breath. 'That's better! One couldn't hear oneself think in that place! Who is Briggs, father?'

'He's t' head overseer, lass. He'll show thee around t' mill. I've business to see to i' Huddersfield and I mun be off. Take care now, not to get too near t' machines. Tha can get thy arm ripped off i' one o' them if tha aren't careful.'

Jess looked up from his machine a second and saw Denshaw re-emerge from the office and make for the outer door. So he was leaving. But his daughter, that pretty dark-haired lass with a bloom about her, was still here. Jess had noticed how well-fed and contented she looked, and well-turned out in her fine sprig muslin gown and worsted cloak. And well-shod too. No problem in the Denshaw's house about getting dainty shoes for a lass's feet. He felt a pang of envy, and reproached himself. It wasn't for his own sake he felt jealous, he told himself, only for the comforts Denshaw could give his children that Jess could never give to his.

A small child with red-rimmed eyes nearly as large as her face looked up into Jess's face earnestly. 'What o'clock is it, Master Drake?' she shouted, her shrill treble rising above the din of the machines.

'It's just struck eleven on t' church clock.'

Her face crumpled. 'It's still a great while till drinking time then,' she said.

'Aye, and tha'd better get back to thy piecing afore t' overlooker straps thee again,' Jess counselled. He'd seen Briggs leathering her furiously some hours earlier when she'd arrived late for work, and no doubt if she fell asleep over her work later in the day, as the little ones often did, he'd leather her again.

The child nodded apathetically and went back to her work. Just in time, Jess thought, for at that moment Briggs appeared, red-faced and scowling, and a few paces behind him Maria came in and went to the far end. Jess had noticed she was missing when he'd sought Briggs earlier for Master Denshaw but thought now only of delivering his message to the overseer. He beckoned him, fearing to leave his loom untended.

'Master Denshaw's brought his daughter – she's in t' office waiting for thee,' he shouted.

'Oh, aye, right,' said Briggs, a flicker of a strange, apologetic kind of smile crossing his face, and he went into the office. Some time later he reappeared with Denshaw's daughter, and Jess saw him conducting her around, pointing and putting his face close to her ear while she inclined attentively towards him to listen.

Long after she had gone, late in the afternoon when Briggs and his two assistant overseers were being kept hard at work with their straps to keep the small children awake, Jess's head jerked up quickly from his machine when a piercing scream ripped through the noise-laden air. It was a hideous noise, far different from the cry of a child being whipped. A flurry of rags hurtling round and round on a distant machine caught his eye but he could not leave his own machine on the instant. Young Ramsbottom came to his elbow.

'I'll take over – go and see if tha can help,' he said.

Jess moved round the machines. People stood looking helplessly at a bundle of rags and blood on the mill floor. Briggs crashed angrily into the group.

'How the hell did this 'appen?' he demanded.

A woman whined with fright. 'I think her foot must a got caught in t' strap, Master Briggs,' she moaned.

Jess felt sick. Suddenly he realised the mess on the floor was all that remained of the little lass who'd asked him the time earlier. He pictured her whirling round and round on the machine, her brains being dashed out on the filthy floor, and he

36

retched.

'Careless fool!' roared Briggs. 'Master Denshaw is not going to be pleased about this, I can tell thee. Ramsbottom! Go tell her mother what's 'appened. Now back to work, all on thee.'

Jess steadied himself and felt a flood of pity surge through him. Poor mother! He knew she counted on the child's two and sixpence to help feed her brood, and his heart bled to think of what this news was going to do to her.

'Tha heard me – back to work, Drake!' snapped Briggs, so Jess returned to his machine. Inside he was burning with indignation at the injustice of it all, and with pity for the suffering of innocents. Another young life snuffed out and no more thought spared for it than for the snuffing out of a candle, for it happened so oft these days in the mill and the mines. Children's lives were cheap. Many more waited hungrily at the mill gates, anxious to fill their places.

Something should be done to right the wrongs these children suffered, and their parents. If only there was some way to help them!

Three

Josiah Denshaw wiped his mouth and fingers on the linen napkin, tossed it on the table, pushed back his chair and belched satisfyingly.

'Eeeh, that were a right good meal,' he said contentedly, ignoring the reproving look on his daughter's face. 'If there's owt I really enjoy it's a bit o' good old roast beef.'

Robert was already ensconced in a deep armchair toasting his toes by the fire. His father sank gratefully into the chair opposite him while Susannah lit the candles and drew the heavy curtains.

'Well, lad,' said old Denshaw cheerfully, 'did our Sukey tell thee all about t' mill then? Has she told thee how impressed she is wi' it?'

'I did not, Papa.' Susannah's voice was cool and distant. She finished arranging the folds of the velvet curtains and came to stand before him. 'I did not, because I was far from impressed with what I saw there.'

'Not impressed? By t' best run mill in t' Colne Valley?' Denshaw could hear the strangled surprise in his own voice. 'Didn't Briggs tell thee about our trade then, how many bolts we deliver – on time, mark you – to t' Cloth Hall every week?'

'To be sure he did, Papa, but he could not explain away those starving, deformed creatures who operate your machines. Nor why they were beaten and cruelly treated. You should not allow such things to occur in your mill.'

Denshaw's anger rose to the accusation in her voice. 'How dost tha mean, starving?' he challenged. 'It's nowt to do wi' me, lass, if they're underfed! I pay fair wages, and it's not my concern if a man drinks his money away instead of giving it to his wife for food!'

'But they have little time to eat while they are working,' Susannah protested. 'Half an hour drinking time, they call it, at midday if they're lucky, and that's all the break they get in a fourteen hour day. How can a child endure that, and being strapped as well? Couldn't you arrange for them at least to be fed in some way?'

'Fed? How?'

Susannah turned and looked away impatiently. 'Oh, I don't know. Arrange for some soup and bread to be given them for breakfast perhaps.'

Denshaw nearly exploded. 'Soup? And bread? Tha doesn't know what tha's talking about, lass. Dost know price o' bread these days?'

'We have plenty, and to spare.'

'Aye, but we're different. Dost know price o' grain? A hundred and fifty-five shillings a quarter, that's what it costs. And tha expects me to feed all them wi' bread? Tha's going out of thy head, Sukey. I'm not made o' brass.'

'But you can't expect them to work on empty stomachs,' Susannah protested. 'Such long hours too. It's inhuman.'

'I'm doing no more nor no less nor any other employer in t' district.'

'But that's what I'm saying, Papa. You could do more. Have you heard of Robert Owen?'

Denshaw considered, rubbing his chin. 'No, I can't say as I have. Millowner, is he?'

'Yes, in Scotland. He's built new houses for his workers and set up a nursery school for the workers' children. He won't let children under ten work in his mills, yet I saw little ones no more than five years old in your mill.'

'More fool him. The young 'uns cost less

40

wages nor t' bigger ones.'

'But he cares about his workers, don't you see, Papa? He gives them conditions that make work worthwhile. He ensures that they get paid even if trade becomes slack and there's no work for a week or two. He won't have overseers with straps in his mills, belabouring children, because he doesn't believe in corporal punishment.'

Denshaw thought about this for a moment. 'Can't see how the fellow makes a profit then,' he commented. 'Anyhow, how did tha come to hear about him?'

'I read it in the *Mercury*, Papa, and I strongly advise you to consider taking similar steps!'

Denshaw snorted angrily. 'I'll do no such thing!' he roared. 'And as I've told thee afore, leave t' *Mercury* and politics alone! It' nowt to do wi' women!'

Robert woke from his reverie at this point. 'Really, Father, you professed yourself delighted this morning that Sukey at least was taking an interest in the business.'

'But not if she's going poking her oar in where it's not wanted!' shouted his father. 'Meddling, interfering women! There's no room for sentiment i' business and the sooner she learns it the better. Robert Owen indeed! He can do what the devil he likes up

41

there i' Scotland and ruin hisself for all I care, but 'ere in t' Colne Valley I know what's best for Denshaw's, and I'll manage it my way.'

'Of course you will, Father, and very efficiently too, if I may say so,' Robert reassured him. 'You've done very well for us up to now and I'm quite happy for you to continue to run the mill as you are doing.'

'Just so long as you don't have to lift a finger,' Susannah snapped. 'Don't you care about the wretched lot of these poor people then?' she demanded.

Robert shrugged his shoulders. 'It is destiny, my dear sister. They were born to be poor. It is their lot, just as it is ours to be wealthy.'

'And what if you had been born poor, one of them?'

Robert smiled complacently. 'But I wasn't, was I? Nor were you, my pet. Be content that Providence saw fit to make you be born into money.'

Susannah turned away with an exclamation of irritation. 'You just don't understand, or care, either of you. I wonder the workmen don't band together against such unfeeling creatures as you.'

'They can't. We've been protected against that,' Denshaw told her. 'Combination Act.

Makes it illegal for men to band together to try and impose conditions on their masters.'

'But that's unfair! How else can they better themselves if you won't help them?'

Susannah's cry of protest was interrupted by a knock at the door. Old Hannah bustled in, bobbed a curtsey and told Master Denshaw that Briggs was waiting in the hall to speak to him.

'At this time on a Saturday night?' old Denshaw said in surprise. 'But t' mill's shut for t' weekend. What can it be?'

He hurried out after Hannah and returned a few moments later. 'Just another little mishap at t' mill this aft,' he said, relapsing into his chair. 'Child caught in a machine. Dead. Remind me to send ten shillings to t' mother will you, Sukey?'

Susannah stared at him in horrified amazement.

'And I might tell thee that's good deal more than most employers'd do in t' situation,' Denshaw added, and picking up his newspaper he prepared to dismiss the incident from his mind.

'Dear God!' Susannah muttered, as if to herself. 'Just as casually as that! If I were you, Papa, I'd be afraid for the consequences.'

'Consequences? What consequences?'

43

'If you can treat people's lives and livelihoods as if they were of no account like that, I'd be afraid of growing resentment and possibly one day some kind of action in retaliation. I wouldn't sleep easy at nights.'

'That's enough,' the old man rasped. 'Get off to bed, Susannah.'

Susannah swept from the room, but there was no obedience in her action. Robert smiled lazily. 'Our Sukey has a will of her own, I'd say, Father. A chip off the old block.'

'Aye, mayhap. But she touched me on a sore point. I've a feeling there's summat afoot, and I don't like t' feel of it at all.'

A flicker of interest crossed Robert's face. 'Something afoot? In what way, Father?'

Denshaw hesitated. 'I don't rightly know. I can't quite put my finger on it, but I've a feeling there's summat going on as I don't know about. Mayhap someone's got to hear about t' frames I've ordered. New cropping frames'll put a good many handcroppers out o' work and it could be they're planning summat.'

'What can you do about it, Father? You could warn the magistrates, perhaps.'

'Aye, but I know nowt for sure. Best to protect t' mill against possible attack, I'm thinking.'

'Call in the military, you mean?'

'Aye, and more nor that. I'm thinking of setting up cannons inside t' millyard wall.'

'Cannons? Sukey will tear her hair!'

'Sukey'll not know. Meddling wench! I'll have to get shut of her if she's going to keep on vexing me over t' workers like this. Marry her off or summat. Trouble is, there's no one as I know on as'll suit her hereabouts.'

'Then let me take her to London with me, Father. There she'll be out of your way and there's a chance she could meet a good match amongst my acquaintances too. A titled gentleman even.'

Denshaw eyed his son thoughtfully. 'I'm not so daft as tha thinks, lad. I know tha wants to get back to London by hook or by crook, but tha's not using Sukey as a pretext. It's not five minutes since I settled thy last lot of gambling debts, and I'm not sending thee back to run up more.'

Robert opened his eyes wide in feigned innocence. 'It's you I'm thinking of, Father, and Sukey too. You've just said there's no one suitable for a match for her here. Now in London...'

'I know, I know. But I've too many problems on my plate just now to worry about that. I've got to get them frames in soon and secretly. That's enough to worry about

45

for now.'

'And with Sukey out of the way, she won't be able to harass you, Father.'

'Leave it alone, lad. After t' frames are safely in, we'll talk of London again, but not tonight. Now I'm for bed. I've had a heavy day.'

So saying old Denshaw levered himself wearily from his chair and made for the door. 'Women!' he muttered to himself as he went. 'Interfering women! But I've a suspicion she's right, and somehow summat is brewing.'

Saturday night was a busy one at the Warreners public house and Joss Armitage, the innkeeper, was kept busy rushing about, red-faced, to serve his customers. As Jess strode into the inn's warmth out of the darkness of the moor he had to search among the seated drinkers to find the face he sought. Mellors had promised to be here tonight with Walker and Thorpe and the others, and Jess was anxious to learn more about the Luddites from this lively young man of action.

He finally spotted Mellors' curly flaxen hair and bottle green coat in a corner. Mellors was leaning forward on a settle talking with great animation and a great deal of gesturing with his hands to a pale young man, a stranger. Jess made his way through to them. Mellors glanced up as Jess's shadow fell on him.

'Evening Drake,' he said with a warm smile, pushing up to make room for him on the settle. 'Friend o' mine – Jess Drake, William Hall of Liversedge.'

Jess and the pale youth nodded to each other, Jess turned back at once to Mellors. 'I want thee to tell me more about these Luddites,' he said quietly. Even so, Hall heard him and glanced sharply at Mellors. Mellors laughed.

'Never fear,' he said to Hall. 'We've another likely volunteer here for twissing in, I'm thinking.'

Hall rose to his feet. 'Well, I see tha's business to see to, and it's getting on. I'd better be off home to Liversedge.' He shook Mellors warmly by the hand. 'I'll tell all my mates down at t' Shears Inn that they've got t' backing o' t' Huddersfield men, shall I?'

'To a man,' replied Mellors. 'If there's owt we can do to teach thy Mr Cartwright a lesson wi' his Rawfolds mill, we'll do it.'

'Tha'll bring John Walker and Tom Brook over to t' Shears to speak to us then, to tell us about t' Luddite movement?'

'Tha can be sure o' that,' Mellors replied.

Such firmness, such assurance the man had! Jess felt warmed just to be near a man with such vigour and decisiveness. He was so much younger than Jess in years, but so much maturer in his self confidence.

Hall nodded and left. Mellors turned to Jess. 'Tha'll come to Liversedge and listen to Walker and Brook wi' us, won't tha? They'll tell thee more about t' Luddites nor I can.' He looked at Jess closely. 'What is it, lad? What's bothering thee?'

When Joss Armitage had plumped their glasses of ale before them and gone away, Jess started speaking, slowly and stumbling a little, for he barely knew himself what ailed him. The story of the little lass caught in the machine tumbled out, and all Jess's heartfelt concern for those in the mills, and especially the children.

'I see,' murmured Mellors when Jess finally came to a halt. 'Then tha'd best come to Liversedge o' Tuesday. Tha'll find t' Luddites feel as strongly as thee about t' bairns, and plan to do summat about it.'

'Then I'll be there,' promised Jess.

Maggie was sitting before a dead fire when he walked home across the moor. She looked up wearily as he came in and went on patting the baby in her arms.

'Maria in yet?' Jess asked, pausing before

he locked the door.

'Aye, she's just back and gone to bed.'

Jess locked up and came across to her. 'How's our Seth then?' he asked, pulling back a corner of the shawl to look at his infant son.

Maggie jerked the child away. 'Leave him be, wilt tha? He's been wakened and fretful all night and I've only just gotten him off to sleep.'

Jess's hopes faltered. 'Is he poorly then?'

Maggie sighed. 'Hungry, that's all.'

It had not occurred to Jess that a babe still at the breast could be hungry. He had thought it would be some time yet before they would have to worry about finding food for him.

'I've not enough milk for him, that's what it is,' said Maggie in a flat voice.

Jess felt a rush of concern. 'Tha's been going without to make sure t' rest of us ate!' he said accusingly. 'Tha mun eat, lass, for t' babby's sake.'

'I know.' There was no feeling in her voice. It was the flat, emotionless tone of a woman who had lost all hope. Jess felt a surge of love and tenderness for her flood his veins.

'Come on, lass,' he said. 'Let me take him while tha has summat to eat. There's still some oatcake up in t' reel.' He reached for the basket over the mantelshelf.

'Leave it be, for t' lasses in t' morning.' Maggie's voice was stern and uncompromising. Jess's hand faltered and fell.

'But tha mun eat, lovey,' he urged her. He remembered he had a message of hope for her. 'Listen to me, lass. Things'll not always be so bad. I've met some men at t' Warreners, and they've been telling me...'

'I'm none concerned wi' your mates' talk,' Maggie said in a tired voice. 'I'm that weary, Jess. I mun go sleep now.'

'But let me tell you, Maggie.'

'Another time, Jess. Not now.'

Jess watched her drag her feet listlessly as she went through into the other room. Ah well, he'd tell her later. Meantime, it was something to hang on to, a hope to hug to himself.

Four

Abigail was walking precariously along the drystone wall that separated one field from the next, her fair hair streaming in the breeze and her thin arms extended to

50

balance herself. All her concentration was focused on her task. Jess, lying on a mound of springy heather not far away watching her, his head propped on his hand, rolled over so as to survey the view of the valley below.

It was Sunday. For one day of the week the mills lay idle, their machines stopped and deserted, and it seemed to Jess that the valley reverted to its erstwhile peace, as in the days before the machines had come. No throbbing sound filled the air, only the song of the birds and the sound of the Colne waters rushing by, for once relieved of their duty of turning the great water wheels. Here and there cottages like his own buried themselves into the moorside as if for maternal warmth, and beyond them the Pennine mountains rose one behind the other, mist-shrouded and purple-grey. Low drystone walls criss-crossed the lower slopes like knotted veins in an old man's hands. Up beyond Denshaw's mill he could see the dam holding back the smooth, expressionless waters of the dam. The might of the Colne, like the might of the valley folk, was repressed and pent up for the rich man's needs.

In the April sunlight the air was heavy with peace. This was how his valley was meant to be, he reflected. This was how it was in the old days, when weavers worked in their own cottages and contentment, if not luxury, was their lot.

He remembered their own little cottage in the days when Maggie was still young and a light still gleamed in her eye. She had been content to sit in the little kitchen with its sanded floor and ochred walls, winding the weft from the cop on to the bobbins for him to weave at his loom upstairs. It had given him pleasure to hear her humming at her work and to come down and sit on the long settle and watch her. The kitchen had breathed contentment, the sleeve clock in the corner ticking away the sweet hours of their close companionship.

And even at his loom upstairs Jess had been filled with a feeling of peace. All was well with his world. Through the open window he could smell the pots of musk and geranium Maggie had lovingly set beneath the window, and he was his own master, rising with the sun so as to make the most of the daylight hours, and working on until the sun's last rays faded and gloom descended. Then he had come down to Maggie and the bairns and their closeness had defied the world outside. Even in winter when snow and storms beset their tiny rough-hewn cottage, inside there had been warmth and tenderness.

Jess remembered all this sadly. Now his old independence was gone. No more did his donkey carry his own fine cloth to market at the Cloth Hall and Maggie, waiting smiling and open-armed, delight at his success on his return. The donkey had long since gone. Now he had to leave Maggie and home behind, to tend the machines of a rich man who proudly took the cloth to market. Where was the justice in it? How could a man find pride in his work as he once had done?

He smouldered angrily with resentment, not only for himself but for all the valley folk, proud and reserved like himself, who had had to surrender their freedom unwillingly to the new god of machinery. He was proud of his folks who had suffered silently such indignity to their pride. Silently until now, that was. He burned with indignation that the great, majestic river flowing beneath him had also been enslaved to the rich man's greed. This was his valley, his river, his folk! Too great, all of them, to be subjected to the rich man's whim!

Mellors was right. The valley folk had suffered too long in silent acceptance. A rumbling, a stirring could be felt. The time was coming when the millowner would be overthrown. It was right. It was fitting. Puny greed had no right to subjugate the might and pride of the valley. The time had come for action, though in what form he did not yet know.

Jess stirred and rose from his heather couch. 'Come on, lass,' he called to Abigail. 'Thy mam'll have dinner ready by now.'

Abigail jumped down off the wall obediently and ran after him down the moor. Jess's heart swelled to watch his little daughter leaping from stone to stone and dabbling her fingers in a rivulet of mountain water making its way to the Colne. She leapt and danced with the eagerness of youth, as yet not disillusioned. So tiny and fragile she looked despite her eight years. Her white smock fluttered hither and thither, patched but as white as Maggie's rubbing board and dolly tub could make it, for she was a proud woman was Maggie. Like a fairy Abigail looked, if such things there were, Jess thought. Like a summer butterfly, doomed to live but a short summer span.

He shuddered at the unbidden thought and rejected it. Abigail would not live but briefly as his lads had done, not if he could help it. She was the bright little flame in his life that gave it meaning and sparkle, and by

God he'd protect this little one and her innocence!

Already there had been talk in the low raftered kitchen of sending her into the mill, but so far Jess had managed to persuade Maggie to leave her be. He had seen the same sparkling zest for life that Abigail had change first in Maria and then in Jenny to a lacklustre deadness after they'd gone into the mill. Maria had seemed to survive with a careless shrug of her shoulders and a toss of her black mane, but Jenny had drooped so lifelessly they had all but given her up for lost this last winter. She'd coughed and coughed till at last the blood came, and then Maggie had relented and let her stay at home, to die, they'd both believed, Maggie and himself. But Jenny was still with them now the spring had come, pale and weak and uncomplaining. Jess's heart ached to think of how gay and carefree she once had been, just like Abigail now. Just as fair and fragile, loving and innocent. And now she sat like a spectre in the hearth corner, sewing and at only sixteen, awaiting her fate.

It must never happen to Abigail. Inwardly Jess vowed he would protect his little one, his favourite, though he was reluctant to admit even to himself that he could favour one of his children above the others. A swift vision of a battered mass of rags and blood on a factory floor sped into his inner sight, and he rejected it instantly with revulsion. Abigail should never be prey to a vile, mechanical monster clanking relentlessly on, as that wretched little mite had been. His whole being yearned to cradle and protect his little daughter, as he once had yearned for Maggie, down there in Dungeon Wood.

When Jess and Abigail reached the cottage it was Maria who was bustling about preparing the mid-day meal. Jenny, as ever, was sitting sewing.

'Where's thy mother?' asked Jess.

Maria flicked her head towards the other room. 'Lying down. She's not feeling so well, so I've got all the work to do on my own. Honestly, as if it isn't enough that I go out to work all week, and then I have to keep house as well. That one's useless.' She flicked her head angrily again in Jenny's direction.

Jenny looked up, wide-eyed. 'I do what I can, Maria, tha knows that. I'd do more if I could. I am sewing thy shawl for thee where tha said tha ripped it on a bramble.'

'Tha'd be more help if tha could fetch me another bucket o' water from t' pump,'

Maria snapped.

'Easy now, Maria.' Jess's voice was soft and soothing. 'Jenny does what bit she can. How are you feeling today, lovey?' He looked at the younger girl anxiously. She had a high flush about the cheekbones that was unusual in her.

'Middling, father. But me mam's not so well.'

'Did she say?'

'No, she just said she wanted a lie down, but I can tell.'

Maria jabbed a ladle viciously into the stewpot over the fire. 'Other folk can rest, all but me seemingly. Sit and sew, have a lie down or go for a walk on t' moor while I get all t' work done.'

'Tha should be glad of thy health, Maria,' Jess murmured.

Maria clicked her tongue. 'Well, come on,' she said, 'Sit thee down and have thy stew.'

Stew was a fine sounding name for it, Jess thought morosely. Never a bit of meat had they seen for months, and the flavour of the stew was strangely lacking without it. Just a few vegetables grown in the patch outside the door and a handful of Maggie's carefully nurtured herbs. Lawful or not, Jess thought, he'd have to snare a rabbit again before long or their mouths would soon have forgotten the taste of meat.

'Take some to me mam,' Maria ordered Jenny.

'I'll take it to her in a minute,' said Jess.

As soon as she had finished eating, Maria rose. 'I'm off out now,' she said firmly. 'Is me shawl done, Jenny?'

Jenny handed her the mended shawl and Maria put it around her shoulders. She took up a piece of broken mirror from the dressing chest and ran her hands over her hair, smoothing it, then pinched her cheeks and lips to give them colour.

'Where art tha going, lovey?' Jess asked her.

'Out,' she replied, and the door clattered into place behind her. Jess looked at Jenny, and she looked away uncomfortably. He decided against asking her if she knew where Maria was going, for fear of making her feel guilty if she had to tell. Jenny's instinctive obedience to her parents' wishes would oblige her to speak the truth if she knew it.

'I'd like to go back to work, Father.' Jenny's words took him so by surprise, that he stopped with his spoon half-way to his mouth. Abigail went on eating unconcernedly.

Jess paused before he answered, indeed so

long he hesitated that Jenny spoke again. 'Dost tha hear, Father? I'd like to go back in t' mill. I'm well enough now, I'm sure I am.'

Jess looked at her. 'Art tha sure, lass? Tha's been pretty poorly all t' winter.'

'Aye, I'm sure.' She looked away again. Jess sensed that there was something she was holding back.

'What is it, Jenny? Tha can tell me, lovey.'

She looked him full in the face. 'I'm not pulling my weight. Maria says so.'

'What did Maria say?'

'She said I was a – a parasite, I think it was.'

'What's that?' asked Jess.

'She says it's someone who lives off others instead of working for their own living. It's like a tick on a sheep's back, she said.' Jenny's face crumpled and she began to cry. 'So I want to go back, Father. Wilt tha let me come wi' thee in t' morning?'

'We'll see, lass, we'll see.' Jess was too troubled to think clearly. He could understand how the lass felt, but talking it over with Maggie would only make Maggie grunt and agree with Maria. Jenny was too frail for the mill. He must keep her out of it if he could.

'I'll go wi' thee to t' mill,' Abigail volunteered.

'Nay tha'll not.' Jess spoke more sharply than was his wont, and at that moment the door opened and Maggie came through, her eyes red-rimmed and her feet still dragging on the floor.

'Take Abigail down to see t' lambs,' Jess said to Jenny, anxious to get the girls away so he could talk to Maggie alone. They took their shawls obediently and went. Maggie sank into a chair and Jess handed her a bowl of broth.

'I heard Jenny say she wants to go back,' Maggie commented. 'Well why not? She's well enough now. Winter's over, t' days are fine and warm. And two wages is not enough for all of us.'

Jess made no answer. He knew that the combined arguments of Maria, Jenny and Maggie were too much for him to contend with and that he'd be forced to agree in the end. So he took the easiest course and stayed dumb.

'And Abigail...' Maggie began, but Jess cut her short.

His cry, 'No, no,' was involuntary but it carried such conviction that Maggie paused.

'Why not?' she asked. 'She's fit and well old enough.'

'No. At least, not yet. Later, maybe, but

not yet. Jenny's five or six shillings'll see us right enough. We'll not need more, not yet.'

'Have it thy way,' Maggie sighed and handing back the empty bowl, she lay her head back on the chair and closed her eyes.

Monday morning the rain drizzled insistently over the whole of the valley. Josiah Denshaw smiled contentedly. So long as the rain kept coming and filling the river, his water wheel would continue to turn and keep his mill throbbing with activity. Just as well. Plenty of orders still had to be met.

He retied his neckcloth for the third time before he was satisfied with it. Dammit, he was becoming as fussy as young Robert about his appearance. He spent his days strutting about like a peacock and changing his jacket and breeches for gayer ones. A right popinjay the lad was becoming! Neither use nor ornament to anyone!

Susannah swept in. 'Papa, we need another maid – and you need a clean neckcloth,' she added, looking at him critically as he turned to her. She came towards him and began to unfasten the neckband he had taken such pains to tie.

'Leave it be!' Denshaw roared.

'I will not. You need a clean one,' Susannah said firmly. 'I'll go fetch another for you.' As she neared the door she turned. 'Now if we had another maid, I could send her instead of going running and fetching myself. That's what I came to speak to you about. I need a maid.'

'What's wrong wi' Hannah?'

'Nothing is wrong with her. Except that she is growing older and needs more help. And just now she is too busy cooking your breakfast to go running for a neckband. In my opinion we need several maids, for in my position I should have a personal maid of my own.'

'One's enough,' said Denshaw curtly, and saw his daughter smile at her easy victory. 'How much?'

'How much, Papa?'

'Aye, how much'll a maid cost me?'

'Living in or out?'

Denshaw shrugged. 'Nay, that's up to thee.'

'Living out, I'd say thirty shillings a quarter.'

Denshaw made a quick calculation. Two and six a week – roughly what he paid a child in the mill. But living in, there'd be the cost of food too. He mentioned this to Susannah.

'Food, Papa? She could feed her family on the amount we leave untouched,' Susannah pointed out, and Denshaw realised she was shrewd enough, this lass of his. It'd cost him nothing but the two and six. Susannah had a sound head on her shoulders all right. Pity Robert wasn't so canny. Money trickled through his fingers like water.

'Right then,' he said at length. 'Engage a maid.' He need question no more. Susannah was wise enough to pick one that was industrious and grateful for the position. He could safely leave it to her.

'And I'd like to come down to the mill with you again today, Papa,' Susannah added when she reappeared a few moments later with the clean neckband. Denshaw was irritated. She'd start her managing ways again if he wasn't careful.

'Not today, lass,' he said with studied mildness. 'It's blowing a gale and raining too.'

She laughed at his exaggeration. 'It's only rather windy, and who's to feel the rain in the carriage?'

So he found himself reluctantly handing Susannah down from the carriage at the mill gate. A figure stood huddled against the mill wall out of the driving rain, and Denshaw recognised that pale, hollow-cheeked lass of Jess Drake's. Good worker, Drake. Quiet as a mouse, but good worker for all that. The lass used to work in the mill too, but coughing had kept her home ill all winter. She still looked peaky and unfit to him.

She approached them timidly, her shawl drawn close about her head, thin fingers clutching it to her chest. 'Morning, Master Denshaw,' she said. 'Me father bade me ask thee if I could start work in t' mill. I'm fit and strong again now.'

'Tha doesn't look so well to me, lass.'

'But I am, really I am. And,' she lowered her gaze to the ground, 'we need the few shillings I can earn. Me Mam's poorly...'

Denshaw clicked his tongue in irritation. He was accustomed to hearing pitiful tales every time he came near his own mill gate. Sometimes it was parents bringing their children and begging for a place for them as pieceners, sometimes former workers having recovered from illness begging for their old job back, all with plaintive tales of need. But all that mattered to Denshaw was to keep his looms rolling, and the cheaper the labour, the better.

The lass was still gazing at him with beseeching wide eyes. Denshaw sighed. 'I'll ask Briggs if he needs anyone,' he relented.

'I'll give you a position.' It was Susannah's voice. Denshaw looked at her sharply. 'I have need of a maid up at Brackenhurst,' she said to the girl. 'How would that suit you?'

The girl's pallid face lit up. 'Living in – I'll pay you twenty shillings a quarter,' Susannah went on crisply. 'Is it agreed?'

The girl nodded. Denshaw was speechless with surprise. The affair was settled and the girl was scuttled away before he found his breath to speak.

'No point in discussing it, Papa,' Susannah cut short his expostulations. 'We need a maid, and I have a fancy she will suit us admirably. I have already sent her to collect her belongings and move in, so the matter is concluded.'

She turned away to enter the mill. Denshaw shrugged. She was a masterful one all right, was Susannah. She knew what she wanted and went right after it. She was decidedly his daughter, and he smiled ruefully, but with deep satisfaction. If only she'd been a lad!

Five

Maggie was not as pleased as Jess had hoped about Jenny's good fortune. She sat on the rush-bottomed chair by the fire, her lips taut and her eyes unsmiling as he told her about Miss Susannah's kind offer.

'I know all about it,' Maggie said in a tight voice. 'Jenny came home, picked up her few belongings and left again as fast as she could.'

Jess could see Maggie was hurt at Jenny's apparent thoughtlessness and her haste to leave their miserable cottage.

'But sithee, lass, she'll be far better off at Brackenhurst,' Jess said soothingly. 'She'll be warm and well-fed, well out o' t' way of t' dust and noise in t' mill. Tha knows it were t' mill dust 'at gave her that cough. 'Appen she'll start to mend now, and afore long she'll be the strong, bonny lass she used to be.'

'Aye, 'appen,' said Maggie tartly. 'But Maria'll have summat to say.' No doubt of that, thought Jess. Maria would be jealous of her sister's fortune. 'Maria'll point out what tha seems to have forgotten,' Maggie went on. 'Jenny's money'll come nobbut once i' three months, not the five or six shillings a week tha promised.'

Jess had not thought of that, it was true, but to him it seemed that Jenny's health should be considered before the money, however desperately the money was needed. He felt vaguely unhappy that Maggie should not view it in the same light.

'Tha'rt soft in t' head,' murmured Maggie sulkily. 'Tha'll put sentiment afore our need. Someone's got to have sense i' this house if tha can't.'

She picked up the baby from his cradle as a thin wail cut into the quiet air. 'Na don't thee start,' she said crossly. She unfastened her bodice and put the child to her breast. Jess noted how thin and flabby her breast was, and his heart ached. The baby sucked feverishly for a few seconds, then let go and began to wail peevishly again.

Maggie set him down in his cradle and sighed, then fetched a jug of milk and began mixing some of it with water and warming it over the fire.

'I'm off out this evening, over to Liversedge,' Jess told her as he watched her.

'Oh?' Maggie replied with disinterest.

'Aye, I'm going wi' George Mellors. I told thee I'd met him and some of his mates at t' Warreners. They think it's about time t' handworkers tried to put a stop to t' mill-owners putting in all these new machines.'

'What use is that to thee?' Maggie asked. 'Thy job were taken over by t' machines a long while back.'

'Aye, but these fellows – Luddites, they call themselves – believe 'at t' landowners and t' factory owners are t' cause of our plight. It's them 'at causes us to starve, and it's time the people took action.'

'I see.' Maggie's voice was still remote, but she was evidently thinking about it. She took up the baby again and began feeding some of the watery blue liquid into his mouth with a broken spoon. The wailing stopped.

'Well, all I can say is, tha'd best take care, Jess. Tha's got a place in t' mill, but if tha does owt foolish, tha could lose it.'

'I'll be careful,' he assured her. 'But I mun get ready now or I'll be late for t' meeting.' He stood by the door, wrapped in his coat and muffler. 'Well, I'll be off.'

'And think on, Jess Drake, tha's got a daughter working up at Brackenhurst now. In t' camp o' t' enemy, as you might say.'

'Aye.' Jess turned that over in his mind. 'Aye, so I have. 'Appen I'd better not tell Mellors that,' he said, and lifting the sneck, he went out.

A couple of hours later Jess found himself sitting in the unfamiliar surroundings of the Shears Inn in Liversedge. It was packed with men, all pale and tense, and an undercurrent of suppressed excitement filled the low-raftered room. Jess sat on a bench near the back close to the wall, alongside Mellors and watched the faces of the two young men sitting at the head of the long table in the centre of the room. On the table were two lanterns, a Bible and a human skull.

One of the young men rose to speak, raising his hand to command attention. The excited murmurs died away and all faces turned attentively towards him. 'That's John Walker,' Mellors whispered.

Walker spoke cheerfully, praising the Liversedge men for being lively enough to attend this meeting with the intention of doing something to improve their lot. He assured them that the contingent of Huddersfield men would be prepared to assist them in any action they undertook, then introduced the other man who sat at the table as Thomas Brook.

Brook, who up till then had sat leaning back in his chair, puffing stolidly on his pipe, now laid the pipe aside and rose slowly. He was a sombre-faced man, but Jess noticed how his dark eyes sparkled, reflecting the lantern light as he spoke.

'Gentlemen,' he said, leaning on his fists over the table and regarding them all earnestly, 'you do not need me to remind you of the lot of the working man today, nor to tell you, who know of it already, of the oppression and hardships the working man must suffer at the hands of his masters. Decent, hardworking fellows all, honest and God-fearing, and now they find themselves about to be put out of employment through no fault of their own. And what do they find? There is no pity or mercy for them anywhere. Those who would put you out of work, my friends, do not wish to be reminded of your existence by seeing the plight you suffer, starving and workless, and your children crying in hunger about you, so what do they offer? Emigrate, they say, get to the colonies, out of our sight!'

He paused momentarily to let his words sink in, and then continued. Jess saw the haggard faces about him furrow in resentment and heard the approving murmurs. After some minutes Brook came to the climax of his speech. He raised his hand.

'You do not need to be reminded of what our children must suffer, God help them, poor innocent victims! You have seen your little ones fade and droop, from lack of food. You have seen them pine and die. Are we to let this go on?'

Angry murmurs were punctuated by spats of oath and blasphemy. Brook's voice rose above the others. 'It is man's right to earn an honest living!' he cried. Jess could feel the surge of emotion and pent-up resentment swelling around him. A burly, sandy-haired man near him wiped away a tear. 'I buried my fourth this aft,' he murmured by way of apology.

'It is the machines that have caused all our misery!' Brook's voice cried, to roars of approval. 'We must get rid of this vicious menace in our midst. We must organise ourselves, military fashion, and seek to sweep these hated machines away!'

It took Walker and Brook some moments to restore a semblance of order to the meeting, so heated and enraged the frustrated listeners had become. Walker coaxed the men to listen attentively to what Brook had to suggest. Brook then spoke more quietly and urgently to the silently eager crowd.

'Cartwright has installed several of these

71

cropping frames already, as you know, robbing the handcroppers of a job. But now I hear as two more wagon loads of frames are to be delivered to his Rawfolds mill this very week. Are you going to let this happen? Are you going to let yet more work be stolen from you?'

Hoarse cries of denial met his challenge. Brook flung up his arms, 'Now is your time then, men! If you want to stop the filching of bread from your mouths, resolve here and now that these accursed machines will never cross Hartshead Moor!'

Loud, enthusiastic cheers acclaimed his proposal. Men jumped to their feet and called out that they were willing to do aught to prevent Cartwright getting his frames in. One of the Huddersfield men leapt up and shouted above the din, 'And we'll bring Enoch – he'll see to t' frames!'

Jess turned and faced Mellors, shining-eyed and silent. 'Who's Enoch? Is he another of the group?'

Mellors laughed at Jess's ignorance. 'Enoch is our great ally, lad. He's a hefty sledgehammer, named after t' blacksmith who made him, and he's been the death of many a machine already. You'll meet him soon enough, if you've a mind to join us.' He looked at Jess quizzically. 'How about it, lad?'

Jess felt shaken and stirred at all he'd seen and heard. Already he could see anxious men were clamouring about the table where Walker and Brook sat, eager to volunteer their services and take the Luddite oath. Mellors sat eyeing him thoughtfully.

Jess cleared his throat and murmured, 'Aye, well, like I said, I don't think much on violence and destruction for its own sake, but like that chap said, there's the bread being taken from our children's mouths, and...'

'Aye, that's right, I knew that'd see it,' said Mellors cheerily, clapping him on the shoulder. 'None of us wants violence, but matters have got that far, what else is there? Within reason, of course,' he added, seeing Jess's stare. 'Come on, let's have thee take the Oath of Fraternity and be wi' us.'

Jess let himself be led, not unwillingly, to the table.

'Add another name to thy list, Mr Brook,' said Mellors. 'Jess Drake, o' Marsden.'

The sombre face looked up at Jess. 'Glad to have you with us,' said Brook. 'In a moment we'll take the Oath. Any more names?'

The final names were listed. An air of suppressed excitement and anticipation of

action to come gave the ragged men an un-
wonted animation. They no longer looked
the dreary, defeated men who had slunk
into the room an hour earlier. Jess awaited
the oath-taking ceremony with a growing
conviction that he had made the right
choice, to help to alleviate the lot, not only
of his own family, but also of all these
splendid Colne Valley folk he loved so well.
He was proud to be at one with them in
their cause. It was an ennobling feeling,
rather reminiscent of the sermons the
minister used to preach in the days when
Jess and Maggie used to go to chapel sometimes, all about goodness combatting evil,
right standing up against injustice.

'Right,' said Brook at last. 'All new members will now take the Oath. Please come
out here in turn and repeat after me what I
say.'

A body of men stood and moved forward,
Jess amongst them. 'Good lad,' he heard
Mellors murmur, and warmed to his approval. Soon it came to Jess's turn. Brook
gave him the Bible to hold.

'Now, start with your own name. I...'
Brook commanded.

'I, Jess Drake,' muttered Jess.

'Of my own voluntary will.'

'Of my own voluntary will.' Jess could see

74

the haggard faces in the flickering lantern light, all intent and deadly earnest as they listened to him swear the compromising oath.

'Do declare and solemnly swear ... that I never will reveal ... the names of the persons who compose this secret committee ... their proceedings, meeting, places of abode, dress, features, complexion, or anything else ... that might lead to a discovery of the same ... either by word, deed, or sign ... under the penalty of being sent out of the world ... by the first brother who shall meet me ... and my name and character blotted out of existence ... and never to be remembered but with contempt and abhorrence ... and I do further swear ... that I will use my best endeavours ... to punish by death any traitor or traitors ... wherever I can find him or them ... though he should fly to the verge of nature ... I will pursue him with unceasing vengeance ... So help me God, and bless me to keep this my oath inviolable.'

Brook nodded. 'Now kiss the Bible,' he commanded. Jess did so, then returned to his place and sat down shakily, troubled by the violence and intensity of his oath, but felt calmed by Mellors' reassuring murmurs. Distantly he heard Brook still talking, about the few coppers a week every member was expected to contribute to the fund, to be used to defend any member who became involved with the law or to support the families of any who were sent to prison. Then he spoke of buying firearms and ammunition. Jess came to his senses quickly.

'Firearms?' he said to Mellors. 'I thought your people did not believe in unnecessary violence?'

'*Our* people,' Mellors corrected him. 'But how else can we carry out attacks on mills if we're not armed? Most mills are defended by the military these days, and they are well armed.'

'But we're not attacking a mill. Destroy t' frames as they come across t' Moor on t' wagons, that's what Brook said,' Jess protested.

'Mills'll come soon,' Mellors promised. 'Mark my words.'

The rest of the evening passed quickly, detailed plans being explained for the attack on Hartshead Moor. At the end, Brook urged members to leave the Shears Inn in twos and threes at a time, so as not to arouse suspicion.

William Hall came up to Mellors and Jess as they were leaving. 'Thanks,' he nodded briefly to Mellors. 'Reckon we'll get our own Liversedge Court of Ludd set up now.'

Jess strode home across the fields towards Marsden alongside the silent Mellors. Jess too was immersed in thought. A vague flicker of conscience disquieted his mind, but as he could not pinpoint its origin, he thrust it out and revelled instead in the feeling of noble endeavour, of union with his fellow sufferers in a joint venture to better their lot. Maggie would be proud of him. A sudden thought provoked him to break the companionable silence between himself and Mellors.

'Why Luddites?' Although he spoke in a low voice Jess was aware that the sound broke into the silence like a pistol shot. Mellors jerked his head up.

'Why what?'

'Why are we called Luddites? It's a strange name.'

Mellors shrugged his shoulders as he strode on, hands deep in his pockets. It was chilly even for April. 'None knows for sure,' said Mellors after a pause. 'Some say there was a fellow in t' stocking mills i' Leicester, a simpleton named Ned Ludd, as smashed up a frame when a gang o' lads tormented him, just to vent his wrath, like. Then when t' Luddites started smashing frames in t' cause, they said when they were asked that Ned Ludd must a done it.'

Jess nodded understandingly. 'I see. But Mr Brook said summat about General Ludd in his speech tonight. Who is this general?'

The younger man smiled knowingly. Jess thought it seemed odd that a man so much younger than himself, barely twenty-two or three, should know so much more than himself. Sharp, shrewd fellow, this Mellors.

'General Ludd,' Mellors explained, 'is the name given to t' man who leads his local Luddite group, whoever he is. That way secrecy is preserved. And all decisions a local group makes are taken at what we call a court of Ludd. Dost see now?'

Jess nodded again, and tried hard to digest all this new information.

'So yon William Hall who called this meeting at Liversedge tonight'll no doubt be Liversedge's General Ludd, do you see?' Mellors went on.

A thought came swiftly into Jess's mind. 'And who's our general?' he asked. 'Who's General Ludd i' Huddersfield?'

Mellors turned and faced him, and in the moonlight Jess could see the broad smile on his youthful face.

'I am,' he said.

Six

In the days immediately preceding the attack on the frames on Hartshead Moor, Jess grew more and more restive. Now he was committed to the cause he was eager for the action to begin. Incidents in Denshaw's mill also caused him to grow increasingly angry about the cruelty and injustice of millowners, not old Denshaw in particular, but all propertied landowners and factory owners who could thus grind down the helpless poor.

He began to notice events which had eluded him before, or he had been too apathetic to notice or care about them. He noticed now how their half-hour 'drinking' time at noon was more often than not curtailed by Briggs pushing the clock on by ten minutes or more; he became more aware of the overseer's use not only of the strap but often of the heavy billy roller, an iron bar two or more yards long and spiked at the ends, to punish unwary offenders. He noticed Briggs's new method of punishing sleepy children by making them stand on one leg on a stool, holding a heavy bar above their heads and strapping them when they let their weary arms lower even a fraction of an inch. And he raged inwardly.

'What's up with thee, lad?' he asked a dirty little urchin sobbing bitterly during drinking time.

'Mester Briggs hit me on t' head wi' a billy roller, and me head hurts something awful. And I can't see properly,' wailed the child. Next day the lad was not at his loom, and Jess heard later that he had just managed to crawl home to die.

All these events mounted up in Jess's mind to terrible, incontrovertible evidence as to the capitalist's inhumanity to his fellow men, and he wondered how he could have been so blind in the past. Thank God Jenny at least had been spared this! He looked sadly at the young girls at their looms with their twisted, deformed legs which would never grow straight again, and marvelled afresh at Maria's resilience. Maria. He looked down the long chamber and saw she was not at her place. And Briggs was missing again.

On the night before the attack Jess met Mellors at the Warreners. Mellors introduced him to a dark-haired youth with a gentle voice.

'John Booth,' said Mellors. 'His father's t' vicar at Lowmoor and a master cropper too.'

The young man, who was no older than Mellors, smiled gravely and put a pale, soft hand into Jess's brown, horny one.

'He's a scholar too,' added Mellors proudly. The youth smiled.

'I am pleased to meet you, Jess Drake,' he said quietly. Jess noticed his thoughtful, serious gaze and his pleasant, gentle way of talking, and was impressed. It was reassuring that a genteel man found the Luddites' cause to his taste. 'I'm but lately twissed in to the cause,' he went on, using the colloquial expression for being sworn in to the group. 'I had no sympathy at first with the idea of action and violence, much as I grieved for the poor man's lot. Machine-breaking seemed wrong to me, but Mellors here made me see otherwise.'

'Aye, well,' said Mellors cheerily. 'Tha came into our shop and read out a piece in t' *Mercury* all about t' Nottingham Luddites and said how shameful tha thought it was – I had to tell thee t' other side, didn't I?'

'And well you did,' agreed Booth. 'At length I was able to see your reasoning and

81

put aside my scruples. As I see it, it's either oppression or submission. So now, Jess Drake, I am at one with the Luddites and am anxious to do all I can to improve conditions for the workers.'

Jess liked this man instantly. Moreover his own vague misgivings were assuaged; if such a clever, intelligent man as this could be persuaded by reason and logic that the Luddite cause was just even if it involved violence, then so could Jess Drake.

They sat with their pots of ale and drank in companionable warmth, and Jess felt content. Mellors left first, and then Booth walked part of the way home with Jess who could sense that the youth, much younger than himself though he was, could feel the same growing amity between them. This was a man he liked and respected, and he looked forward to seeing and learning more of John Booth.

They shook hands at the bridge and Jess felt the warm softness of the man's hand in his. Then they parted, to meet again on the morrow for their venture on Hartshead Moor.

Jess slept little that night, tingling with excitement and turning restlessly, trying not to disturb Maggie whose bony back was turned to him as it always was these days.

But he had no time to fret over that as his mind ran on excitedly to what the following night would bring.

At last it came. The night was crisp and clear and the moonlight fell over the vast desolation of Hartshead Moor, retreating occasionally behind a cloud. Jess crouched behind a rock with Booth and Mellors and felt his heart lurching with excitement.

Behind nearby rocks more men crouched, some with blackened faces and some in masks. Hushed voices murmured and hands moved hammers and hatchets to readier positions. Jess felt awed by the darkness and eerie quiet and the weird shapes made by the silhouettes of the craggy rocks. The long, rutted road snaked across the moor below them and away into the distance, and Mellors' eyes were strained in that direction.

It was a long, cold wait. Booth sat silent and deep in thought, as if in prayer. Suddenly Mellors held up his hand and hissed, and the murmurs of the men died away. A faint sound grew slowly into the distinct clop-clopping of horses' hooves on the frosty road. They came slowly closer, and Jess felt himself stiffen with anticipation and his heart fluttered wildly.

'No guards,' he heard Mellors mutter. 'We are in luck.'

The wagons rumbled slowly along the road below, and Mellors raised his hand as a signal. Instantly the men ran in a body down the slope and swarmed over the wagons like ants. Jess watched as in a dream. He saw the drivers pulled from their perches, bound and gagged swiftly and silently, and placed on the roadside.

'Come on,' Mellors' voice urged him, and Jess took up his hammer and fell on the heap of ironwork in the first wagon. He struck and smashed till the frames lay in smithereens, and felt an exultant glow spread through his veins. Booth swung a hatchet alongside him, silent save for hissing intakes of breath.

'Away!' cried Mellors when at last the job was done. The men stopped their work of destruction at once and followed his retreating figure up the slope. Out of sight beyond the rocks Mellors ordered them to disperse in small groups, and they disappeared into the dark.

Jess felt heady as he hastened back to Marsden. As if he had drunk too much, he thought. He glowed and throbbed and wanted to shout for joy. Such a sense of achievement he had, such a feeling of having struck a blow for freedom from oppression, and his heart sang. What was more, Booth had smiled approvingly before he had disappeared into the night. Jess felt his liking for this man grow into a kind of brotherly love, for they were indeed brothers of the heart.

Intoxicated with pleasure and pride in his achievement, Jess held up his head and strode home proudly to tell Maggie.

But Maggie was in bed when he arrived. Maria was still in the kitchen washing dishes and grumbling about having to cope without Jenny's help, but he left her to it and went through into the other room. Maggie lay still but he knew she was not asleep. The baby lay awake but silent.

He undressed and slipped into bed by Maggie, drawing her close to him. 'Listen, lovey,' he said, and told her the tale of the night's doings. Maggie lay listening but made no comment until he had done.

'Aren't tha pleased, lass?' he asked at length.

Maggie grunted. 'Seems to me tha'd be better employed bringing some money home 'stead of smashing up machines.'

'But don't tha see, Maggie, that's only t' beginning on it? T' Luddites want to see food in t' babby's bellies same as we do. This is only t' start.'

'Aye well, best not let Jenny know when

she's home on Sunday. 'Appen Mester Denshaw could come to hear of it if she blabs to someone, and then it'd be t' towzer for thee, and what'll happen to us all then?'

The possibility of prison, or towzer as she called it, had not occurred to Jess. He considered it thoughtfully. 'Aye, 'appen tha's right. Best not speak to anyone, not Maria nor Jenny neither. After all, I'm under a sacred oath not to speak. Oh but Maggie! Such a warm feeling as I had tonight, smashing them frames! I did it for thee, love. I want to make things better for thee!'

He took her close to prove his love for her, but Maggie pushed him off. 'Let me be!' she said shortly.

'But I love thee, lass and tha loves me, I know.'

''Appen. But I want no more sickly bairns to have to watch die, Jess Drake, and that'd be t' consequences. So leave me be.'

She turned away and drew up her knees against her chest with determination. Jess sighed. She was right of course, but he did so want to express his love for her and crown his jubilation over the night's exploits.

He was nearly asleep when he heard Maggie muttering. 'Tha's soft in t' head,' she murmured. 'Any man can make a fool of thee. Smashing frames indeed! If t' magistrate comes to hear on it, we're done for. Tha'rt any man's fool, Jess Drake. Anyone wi' a soft voice can twist thee round his little finger.'

Jess's exultation began to filter away, then he heard her voice add in the darkness, 'And a soft heart too. I know tha loves us, tha soft thing.'

On Sunday Jenny came home for the day. Jess was delighted to see that already a little of the pallor had left her thin cheeks, and there was an unaccustomed light in her hitherto lustreless eyes. He listened to her talking excitedly to Maggie about her new job, while Maria stood with hands on hips, pouting as she listened.

'Hey, what's this?' said Maria suddenly, stooping to lift Jenny's skirts and revealing a pair of clogs on her feet. 'How'd tha come by these?'

'Miss Susannah, she gave 'em me, and said she'd get me a new worsted gown too, for me own's too ragged to be seen in, she said,' Jenny replied, her eyes sparkling with pleasure. 'She's so kind, mam, she really is. She's promised me some old clothes she were going to throw out, for me to bring home. There's a fine jersey shawl as'd be lovely for thee.'

Maggie made no comment, but Maria's dark eyes and pursed lips spoke volumes to Jess. Jenny went on prattling about the fine way of life up at the big house, innocently unaware of the envy and discontent she might cause.

'I've me own bed, wi' woollen blankets on, and they burn coal, not wood, on t' biggest fires tha ever saw. And meat every day.' Her eyes grew wide in recollection. 'And Hannah – she's the cook – says I may bring thee a bit o' roast beef one Sunday if there's some left over. Oh, if only tha could see t' house, mam. It's lovely. Rugs on t' floors, big thick curtains and shining brass and pewter everywhere. And it smells lovely too. Miss Susannah burns some little pellet things in a dish and they make the whole place smell beautiful.'

'What's mester like?' asked Maria quietly.

'Mester Denshaw? He's fair enough, I reckon, though he does shout something terrible. Then there's Mester Robert, but I reckon he's not noticed me yet 'cause he's never spoken. Very fine gentleman he is, real lace on his shirts and all.'

Jess was happy that Jenny was obviously content with her new position but sad to see Maria's ill-concealed jealousy and resentment. Maggie's reaction was more difficult to gauge, for she said little, merely grunting now and again as she listened to Jenny's rapturous account.

But he did not spend long in contemplation, for his mind was still spinning with the activities of the Ludds. He was as anxious as a young lover to meet his energetic young friends again, to jubilate over their recent success and plan the next act of destruction. Impatiently he waited for the next rendezvous at the Warreners.

Josiah Denshaw clapped his son enthusiastically on the shoulder. 'Ah've done it lad! The frames are in!' he cried.

Robert regarded his father with a lazy look of indifference. 'Done what, Father?'

'The frames, lad, they're in t' mill, wi'out anybody knowing, not even thee! I've cheated them Ludds, blast 'em, they never knew owt about it. Got 'em in during t' night, I did. And now there's cannon in t' yard to defend t' mill and t' military is going to patrol every night.' Josiah chuckled with pleasure at his own cunning and rubbed his hands together. 'So much for the Luddites' threats. They'll learn they can't master me. A Denshaw'll never be cowed by t' likes o' them.'

'Congratulations, Father,' said Robert dryly. 'So now perhaps I can return to London as you promised.'

'London be damned!' his father roared. 'I've too much on me mind to be bothered wi' such as that yet. Come wi' me to t' mill while I give Briggs his orders about t' machines.'

But once again Robert declined. Denshaw found Briggs in his dusty office, going over a sheaf of papers.

'The Ludds are going to be mad about this,' Briggs commented when Denshaw had finished raving ecstatically about his cleverness in getting the frames in in secret. 'I'll wager they'll plan summat in return.'

'Blast the Ludds! They'll never get past my cannon,' Denshaw roared. 'They'll never touch my frames. And if they dare to try, I'll ride up to my saddle girths i' their blood afore I'll let 'em by, Goddam me if I won't!'

He cracked his riding crop viciously across the table where Briggs was sitting, to emphasise his words. Briggs rose and went round him to close the office door.

'Tha should take care what tha say, and where tha says it,' he muttered as he went. 'There's probably Ludds i' this very mill for all tha knows.'

'What do I care? Dosta think to frighten

me? Let 'em all hear and take heed not to try and meddle wi' me, if they know what's good for 'em,' Denshaw shouted defiantly. He wrenched open the office door again and strode into the loom chamber. Briggs hurried after him.

Amid the clatter of the machines Denshaw had stopped by a bench and was looking at Maria. 'That's that lass o' thine,' he said as Briggs caught up with him.

'Not mine – Jess Drake's lass,' Briggs corrected him.

'And thine too, if I'm not mistaken,' said Denshaw with a hint of a smile. 'I'm not daft, tha knows. I've got eyes i' my head. Does thy wife know owt about it?'

Briggs hung his head and did not answer.

'I hear tell as thy wife has been poorly a great while. It'd not do her much good to hear about this,' Denshaw said, and strode to the mill door. There he paused and turned, and raised his voice loud to drown the clacking of the machines. 'Remember what I tell thee, Briggs. Any sign of trouble and tha to let me and t' military know at once. No Ludd is going to better me. I'll fight 'em to t' death. I'd sooner ride up to me saddle girths i' their blood nor see any harm come to my machines.'

He liked the colourful phrase, and wanted

91

every Ludd in the district to hear of it. He strode out of the mill door, content that close on every soul in the loom chamber must have heard him, and those who had not, would soon have his words relayed to them.

He swung himself up into the saddle with a satisfied smile. 'Na then, Briggs, we'll see if any on 'em dares defy me after that,' he said, and cantered out of the mill yard, past the cannon with its nose pointing menacingly through the embrasure in the yard wall.

Seven

Almost nightly that April Jess hastened across the springing heather of the moor to the Warreners, to meet Mellors and Booth and the others. Before he met the young Luddites he had occasionally frequented the Red Lion in Marsden, but now that hostelry rang with the noise and laughter of the rowdy young redcoats billeted there, and Jess deemed it wise to keep well clear of the military now that he was steeped in

Luddite business.

Mellors was crouching over the fire at the Warreners one evening soon after the Hartshead Moor attack. He was engrossed in conversation with Booth and Walker and Thorpe when Jess entered, and Jess could see by his flashing eyes and the agitated movements of his hands that he was excited about some matter. Jess pulled up a chair and sat nearby.

Mellors looked up. 'Good evening, Jess lad,' he said warmly. 'Come nigh t' fire while I tell thee about last night at Halifax.'

Booth smiled a welcome as Jess pulled his chair into the circle, and nodded.

'We had this big meeting, sithee, over at St Crispin's Inn,' explained Mellors, 'and this chap George Weightman were there. Very big chap i' Nottingham he is, organiser for t' Ludds there. He were telling us,' Mellors voice sank to an excited whisper, 'he were telling us that t' Luddite Council i' Nottingham is ready to organise a general uprising all over t' country, a big, concerted effort, like.'

Jess heard Walker and Thorpe's quick intake of breath. 'All over t' country at once?' breathed Thorpe. 'That should make 'em sit up and take notice on us then.'

'Aye, but Weightman said not till t' end o'

May,' went on Mellors. 'I told him we wanted action now, but Weightman said not to be impatient, to wait till everyone was ready to strike at once, but I don't see as we need wait.'

Booth cleared his throat. 'What are you suggesting, George?'

Mellors' eyes gleamed. 'We'll take part in t' uprising next month, of course, but I thought we could be doing summat about local conditions in t' meantime. No point in sitting about idle, is there, wi' all our men drilled and trained to march and strike, and just dying for t' opportunity to act?'

'You're proposing some form of action here locally then, I take it?' Booth asked.

'I am that, lad,' replied Mellors firmly. 'Who are t' local tyrants, tell me? Who are t' millowners causing us most distress? I'll tell thee – Cartwright and Denshaw. And I'm proposing that we attack their mills to teach 'em a lesson.'

His eyes glittered in the firelight with a hard bitterness Jess had not seen before. Booth murmured thoughtfully but Walker and Thorpe muttered 'Aye, why not?'

'I'd like to a started wi' Denshaw,' Mellors said. 'He's vowed to ride i' our blood, but I swear we'll ride i' his first.'

'I do not think personal vengeance is a

94

good reason,' Booth said, coming out of his silence at last. 'I know he has publicly scorned our efforts, but there is no need to hate him.'

'I hate all millowners.' Mellors' voice was sharp with venom. 'And him in particular. Any road, we agreed at t' meeting last night to start by attacking Cartwright's. I hear as Denshaw and Cartwright have both made preparations for defending their mills, but I doubt not the defences have been exaggerated. Properly organised and wi' our weapons, I'm sure we could get in, strike, and away again afore they'd get us. But we mun do it soon if we're to do it at all.'

'Did Weightman agree to the attack then?' asked Booth.

'Aye in t' end. T' others there were i' favour. There's a party o' men fra Leeds coming to help us, and some fra Bradford and Dewsbury too, so we should make a lively party for t' soldiers at Rawfolds to deal wi'.'

Jess could see Walker and Thorpe were growing as excited as Mellors about the new attack. They craned forward in their seats, their eyes gleaming.

'When's it to be, George lad?' asked Thorpe.

'Next Saturday, April eleventh.'

'Where are we meeting, and when?' Booth asked slowly.

'Then tha's coming?'

Booth tapped his fingers together thoughtfully. 'I'll be there, but in some way I don't quite like the feel of it,' he said.

'Tha'll be all right wi' me,' enthused Mellors, clapping him on the shoulder. 'I knew tha'd see reason.'

'Where then, and when?'

'Dumb Steeple, near t' Three Nuns at eleven o'clock,' replied Mellors. 'Tha'll be there too, Jess lad?'

Jess looked at Booth's sober face. If John Booth thought it fitting to join in this new act of violence, then it must be right. He was a learned man, a scholar, and a parson's son at that. If he had turned over the arguments for and against the attack in his mind and judged it right, then there was no point in Jess trying to ponder on the conflict in his own mind. Mellors might be fiery and impulsive, but this man was cool and intelligent and Jess respected his opinion.

'Aye, I'll be there,' Jess said.

'Good lad. Now we'll drink to t' success o' Saturday night,' cried Mellors jovially. 'By heck, we'll give Cartwright summat to think on then. Landlord!'

* * *

96

Every night for the rest of that week Jess had no time for drinking in the Warreners. He spent his nights parading in the fields with twenty or thirty other Ludds under George Mellors' command, drilling and marching, learning commands and how to obey instantly. In the watery moonlight Mellors barked and snapped, then encouraged and commended by turns. Men armed with ancient muskets and hayforks marched and wheeled and stood stiffly to attention at his command. Occasionally the man posted as sentry on a ridge would warn them that the redcoats were in sight, and the men would lie low until the hoofbeats died away over the moor.

At last Mellors declared himself satisfied with the men's demeanour, and said the Duke in Spain could have no finer soldiers than this. Jess felt proud. Booth marched and drilled alongside him, but always in silence and Jess could only wonder what he felt. As they sat side by side on the wiry grass, resting their aching feet after the drill was ended, Jess asked him what he was thinking.

'I'm thinking we'll never have enough arms to overcome soldiers properly equipped,' Booth answered.

Mellors had come up behind them. 'I've

97

seen to that,' he said curtly. 'Groups of Ludds are out this very minute, disguised, banging at people's doors and demanding whatever weapons they've got. Any road, wi' luck, we should be away again afore t' military knows we're there.'

Booth looked up at him. 'You'll put the fear of God in all the cottagers, banging at their doors,' he murmured.

Mellors laughed shortly. 'Not the cottagers. It's only at the bigger houses my men are calling. No one'll dare refuse a band of desperate, demanding men wi' black faces. We'll have arms enough by Saturday, I promise thee. Nowt'll stop us getting into Rawfolds mill.'

Jess grew more and more excited and impatient as the week passed. To Maggie's question 'Where's ta been?' every night when he came home late he simply answered 'Wi' me mates,' and he knew by the shrug of her shoulders that her inflection was, 'Well if tha doesn't want to tell me, I don't want to know.' It wasn't that he didn't want to tell her all the secret joy of anticipation he was hugging to himself; it was simply that he felt the less she knew, the safer she was. No one could prise out of her, either by accident or design, something she did not know.

At last Saturday night came. With the same surge of excitement and pride as on the night of Hartshead Moor, Jess set off to meet Mellors and Booth and the others at the Dumb Steeple. He had to feign sleep till Maggie was safely asleep and then steal silently away into the night, taking with him the sledgehammer Mellors had given him.

He was amazed to see the large number of stealthy grey shadows moving furtively towards the field when he arrived. Over a hundred men, he estimated, must be there already. Some were dressed in carters' smocks and had blackened faces; others wore their coats turned inside out or wore kerchieves over their faces. It took some time to distinguish Mellors from the others, but Jess finally recognised him by the quiet, commanding tone of his voice.

'Thorpe,' Mellors was saying. 'Thee take the pistol company and call 'em over.' Mellors himself then called over his musket men, not by names but by numbers. Jess saw some of the men swigging rum to bolster their courage and others wide-eyed and halting, obviously doubtful whether they should have come.

Booth appeared at Jess's elbow. 'God go with thee, brother,' he whispered. Jess flushed and knew not what to say in reply.

Mellors joined them.

'Bradford and Dewsbury have sent us but a handful of men after all,' he snapped angrily. 'I was counting on five hundred men tonight all told, and there's scarce a hundred here.'

'And what of Leeds?' Booth asked him.

'They're to join us up near Rawfolds. They'll be there, I'll stake my life on it,' Mellors replied. 'But it's a grave disappointment about the others nonetheless.'

'A hundred's enough for a night's bloodshed,' Booth murmured. Mellors looked at him sharply.

'Bloodshed? Why dosta say that, John?'

'You know Cartwright has prepared for such an attack as this. It is unlikely we shall get away without someone coming to harm.'

'That's defeatist talk, lad! Cheer up, we'll be in and away afore they know owt about it,' Mellors exhorted him.

'I hope you're right, George, I truly hope you're right.'

'No more time for clacking, lad, I've to line t' men up. See thee afterwards at t' Warreners.' Mellors strode away.

Jess saw Booth clasp his hands and lower his head and murmur some words that sounded like, 'Into thy hands, O Lord...' Jess felt embarrassed and stood silent. It was a fitting act for a parson's son to pray before battle, and Jess loved him the better for it.

The shrill sound of a whistle pierced the air. It was the signal to fall in, as they had been drilled, in lines two deep. Booth gripped Jess's hand before they fell in.

'I'll see you straight after, and walk home with you, Jess, if God spares us,' he muttered, and was gone.

Three companies of men then lined up, the first carrying pistols, the second muskets and the third hatchets. The remainder of the men including Jess carried sledgehammers or bludgeons. Mellors marched down to inspect each company and as he passed Jess he called two men.

'Hale, and thee Rigge, go march behind the last and see no coward tries to make off in t' dark. If any man tries, shoot him. Now men, forward march! Left, right, left, right...'

The band of men moved quietly forward up and over the moor for three miles or more until they reached a thicket not more than sixty yards from Rawfolds mill. It was well past midnight now. Here they paused while the musket men charged their firearms and final swigs of rum were tossed off.

Mellors was pacing impatiently up and down alongside his men. At last he barked angrily, 'Still no sign of the Leeds men, and they promised to meet us here, damn 'em!'

Hale went, and reappeared some minutes later to say the road was clear for miles, no sign of the Leeds contingent nor sound of their marching feet.

Mellors scowled. 'Well, we can't wait here all night or dawn'll be breaking afore our work is done. We'll have to go in wi'out 'em. Come on, lads!' He formed his musket men into lines fifteen abreast and led the way, Thorpe and his pistol men following him.

Jess's heart thudded with apprehension as he saw them move off. He was in the group of twenty or so hammer men which was to follow in last. His gaze roved over the others crouched near him, but he could not see Booth.

The hammer men turned out of the thicket into the little lane leading down to the mill. Against the skyline Jess could see the buildings, the mill itself and smaller buildings which must be the drying house and the dyehouse, all lined along the banks of a stream which glistened in the moonlight. The great water wheel stood idle. The clump, clump of marching feet was the only sound in the night.

No lights shone in the mill, but the chimney emitted a thin column of smoke.

Jess realised that that did not necessarily signify that anyone was within; only that the boiler fire had been banked up ready to start work again on Monday morning.

Then the fierce yapping of a dog broke into the night air, and following it a light shone out from the counting house window. Mellors' voice rang out, loud and clear.

'Hatchet men forward!' he cried. 'Rush the main gates!'

Eager men leapt forward and crashed their hatchets deep into the wood, and Jess heard it cracking and splintering while the dog's barking grew fiercer and more lights began to glimmer inside the mill.

'Musket men, fire a volley at the windows!' Mellors' voice commanded, and the shots rang out, followed by the sound of crashing glass. 'Keep firing! Use stones or aught you can!' Mellors cried, and Jess saw Booth then, picking up and hurling a large stone. 'Thorpe, take thy group round to force t' other door!' Mellors called again, and a band of men hastened round the narrow footpath alongside the water to attack the further door.

Suddenly the main gate gave way under the bombardment from the hatchet men. 'Forward!' the voice cried, and Jess felt himself carried forward by the streaming flood of men. He felt the cobblestones of the mill yard under his feet and had to duck the cascade of falling glass and flying bricks around him. The hammer lay heavy in his hands.

Muzzles of guns glinted in the upper windows but Jess was astounded when answering streaks of fire cracked at them from within the mill. Bullets whined over him and he heard cries as someone was struck and fell. Voices of men behind him roared and cursed, and the thudding of hammers and hatchets on the door filled the night.

Two men bearing the enormous sledge-hammer they called Enoch pushed Jess aside. 'Make way for Enoch!' one of them cried, and Jess recognised Booth's voice. He rushed forward to help him, and the bodies parted to allow them to pass. Booth swung the hefty hammer with a strength that was amazing for a man not accustomed to manual labour, and when he paused at last, gasping for breath, Jess grabbed Enoch from him and swung it aloft, crashing it on the door and striking sparks from the bolt heads.

The mill bell began tolling, calling for aid from the soldiers stationed nearby. Lime fell from the upper windows on the heads of the attackers beneath. Through it all Jess heard the sound of Enoch thundering on the door. When at last he stopped, breathless, sweating and his heart thudding, someone grabbed the hammer from him and carried on the work. Mellors' voice could be heard above the furore, crying 'Bang up, lads!' and, 'In with you.' After a time the clanging bell ceased. Still the bullets whined around them and fresh cries from the wounded men rang in Jess's ears.

He felt sick and faint, not only from his efforts in wielding the huge sledgehammer, but also with nausea at the terrible scene in which he was taking part. Never had he dreamt the attack could be so awful and so bloody.

George Mellors appeared, his eyes wild and bloodshot. 'We've got to get in at 'em, blast 'em!' he cried. He leapt on a window sill and clawed at the broken glass in the frame, but only fell back with his hands covered in blood.

A voice cried out above the din. 'The soldiers! They're coming, the soldiers are coming!' and at once the men left off their hammering and firing.

Mellors glared angrily in the direction of the mill windows where shots were still issuing, shook his clenched fist and then turned. 'Away, lads!' he called, and Jess could hear the bitter disappointment in his voice. 'Carry the wounded and fly!'

Men bent to retrieve their fallen comrades, and Jess saw Thorpe bending over a tall, dark figure with blood pouring from its leg. Jess moved forward to help him, and saw it was Booth lying prostrate on the ground.

Booth's eyes flickered open. 'Go, while you can,' he murmured. 'I'm done for.'

Without a word Jess and Thorpe took hold of him under the shoulders and dragged him through the slime of his own blood out of the mill yard. Jess dare not look at the shattered leg for his heart was crying out in pity and anger for his friend.

Mellors ordered them to let go and depart. Jess looked at Mellors in horrified silence as Mellors bent to examine the wounds of John Booth and Sam Hartley, who was moaning piteously and coughing up blood.

'I'm right sorry,' said Mellors when he straightened. 'I'm truly sorry, John lad, and Sam, but I think it were best we leave thee. Tha both too badly hurt to move, we cannot carry thee, and we cannot stay when t' military is on its way. We mun go, I fear. Come lads,' he called to the others, and they scuttled off in the dark.

'Come on, Jess,' he urged. Jess stood stock still. Leave his friend in this piteous state? It was unthinkable.

'I'm not going,' he said stoutly.

'Do as you're bid,' Booth whispered. 'There's no point in more of us being caught.'

'I'm not going,' Jess repeated stubbornly.

'Do as tha will,' said Mellors. 'I'm off. But make sure tha both keep mum if tha're questioned, remember. Bear in mind t' Oath tha took.'

'Have no fear,' said Booth faintly. 'Only get away quickly.'

'And thee, Sam,' Mellors persisted. 'Be true to t' cause, lad. Tha must endure.'

Sam Hartley groaned feebly and Mellors took it as a sign of assent, for he nodded and hastened away. 'Come Jess!' he called after him.

But Jess crouched by Booth. 'Go,' said Booth. 'You'll be caught.'

'I'll not leave thee like this,' said Jess stubbornly. He still had to keep his eyes averted from the bloody mess where Booth's leg had been. Looking across at Hartley he could see the blood bubbling in the gaping hole in his chest, and Hartley lay white and still in the moonlight.

Footsteps came clattering across the mill yard towards them.

'For God's sake, hide!' Booth uttered the faint cry and fell back. Jess slipped quickly behind the hedge and crouched low, listening. Lantern lights flickered in the lane.

'Here's one on 'em!' a voice cried as the footsteps approached. 'God, he's in a bad way! Hole as big as my hand through his shoulder.'

'And here's another!' cried a voice just on the other side of the hedge from Jess. 'He's bad too – leg nearly shot off. Reckon he needs a doctor quick!'

'What's going on?' a lower, more commanding voice demanded. 'Have you found some on 'em?'

'Aye, Mester Cartwright, there's two on 'em, badly wounded. They need t' doctor quick.'

'Not till I've done wi' them,' the low voice said. 'Have you seen what they've done to my fine mill? Tell me, fellow, who't leader is brought you all here, eh?'

There was a mutter. 'He says he wants water, Mester Cartwright.'

'Tell me who brought you, blast you!'

No answer. Jess seethed. Could they not see Booth was near unconscious with pain, he thought angrily? Why waste time when he needed help so desperately?

'Why don't they speak? Are they both wounded?' Cartwright asked.

'Aye, sir. Reckon they'll not be able to tell thee owt yet a while.'

'Well they're getting no help from me till they do speak.'

'But they could die afore that. Tha'd best let the doctor see to 'em first.'

Jess smouldered with frustration behind the hedge. It was all he could do not to leap out and fly at the man's throat. Cartwright, that was the man, the mean, greedy mill-owner Mellors had sworn to put out of business, and had failed.

Cartwright grunted. 'Right then,' he yielded reluctantly. 'Get a doctor here, quick as you can.' Footsteps pounded off down the lane.

'Here comes Parson Robertson,' someone called, and galloping hoofbeats echoed in the night. Jess crouched lower as men dismounted in the lane.

'I've brought the soldiers,' a strange voice said.

'Thankee parson,' said Cartwright. 'We've caught two on 'em, pretty badly hurt though.'

'Then they'll need to make their confession,' said the parson, 'in case they're not long for this world.'

'Aye, so I thowt too, but they've passed out.'

It was some ten minutes of agony for Jess, crouched and cramped in the damp hedge-row, before the wheels of a carriage crunched up the lane, and a gentleman descended.

'Doctor Bamforth, there's two men here wounded,' said Cartwright. Jess heard the man stoop to examine first Booth then Hartley.

'Bring me light,' the doctor commanded, then there was a pause. 'Yes,' he said then gravely, 'they are both in a serious condition. This one needs his leg amputated immediately. Take them both to the Star Inn and I'll see to them there.'

'And I'll come too and hear their confessions there,' said Parson Robertson. There was a sound of lifting and grunting, crunching of gravel and moans from the wounded men, then the carriage drove off down the lane. The men left behind began to trickle away to their homes, taking their lanterns with them, and at last Jess was alone in the hedge in the darkness.

When the last crunching footstep had died away, he rose stiffly and stretched his cramped limbs. He felt sick at heart and nauseated. Never had he expected the night to end like this, a night of carnage and bloodshed, and his heart was heavy with guilt for the fate of his friend John Booth. But Booth and Hartley had now been moved to the inn and a doctor was caring for them, so what further use was there in his staying? Best to do as the other Ludds had done, and get away home quickly.

But Jess's legs dragged wearily across the moors, as heavy as his heart. He could still see in his mind's eye Booth praying for deliverance before the battle, and hear him promise to meet Jess after it. Jess could have done no less than wait to see Booth cared for after that. Pray God he would survive and recover.

But as Jess remembered the shattered, pulpy mush which had once been Booth's leg, he doubted it.

Eight

Jess could hardly bear to face Mellors again after that grisly night, but they had all agreed beforehand to meet the following morning at the Warreners to discuss the night's exploit. Jess sat silent, filled with a sense of shame and disillusionment, but Mellors' eyes burned like angry coals as he addressed his men.

'How were we to know t' bolts and studs in t' mill door would withstand Enoch?' he cried. 'I thowt we'd be in and out in no time, 'stead of which we accomplished nowt. And left two men for dead into t' bargain.'

He glowered at them ferociously as if it was their fault, and then added in a mutter, 'Best if they were both dead, Booth and Hartley, for if they live to tell t' tale, its the long drop for us.'

Meaningful looks were exchanged between the men. Jess felt he had to speak. 'They'll not tell tales,' he said quietly. 'They wouldn't answer Cartwright, nor t' parson.'

'How dosta know?' Mellors demanded.

So Jess told him what he had overheard in the hedge. 'At the Star, eh?' said Mellors thoughtfully when he had done. 'Now, if we could get someone in there to keep a watch on what happens...'

Jess looked up eagerly. 'I'd like to go,' he said, 'but how?'

Mellors thought for a moment, then a cunning gleam came into his eyes. 'Booth's a parson's son, isn't he? Tell thee what, tha could pretend to be Parson Booth's verger, sent over by t' father to see how his son is. Everyone knows the old man is too ailing to come himself. Parson Robertson'll not know another parson in Lowmoor's verger, will he?'

It was Mellors' idea, but in spite of the fact that at this very moment Jess felt he could hate Mellors for causing John Booth's tragic mishap, he was willing to fall in with the plan for the sake of getting near Booth and finding out how he was.

It was late morning that Sunday by the time Jess had retraced the miles across the moors to the Star Inn. A soldier in the taproom leapt up from his tankard to demand who Jess was and what his errand, but he seemed to accept Jess's story readily enough.

'T' parson's up wi' Booth now,' the soldier told him. 'T' doctor's just left. He had to amputate Booth's leg earlier today, but I think he's a goner for all that. They can't stop t' bleeding, you see. Parson Robertson's waiting for him to waken, if he ever does. I'll tell him you're here.'

The soldier went and reappeared a few moments later to say Jess could go up, but he was to sit quietly just inside the door and not disturb the two sick men who lay there.

Jess climbed the creaking stairs to the

room he had been told. He knocked very gently and went in. In two beds lay the ashen faces he recognised as those of Booth and Hartley. The parson sat on a chair between the beds, and he signalled to Jess to sit.

Jess lowered his weight on to the chair by the door and sat silent. A clock ticked slowly and remorselessly on the mantelshelf. Nearly noon. John Booth's outline was clearly distinguishable through the sheet covering him, and Jess felt sick to see where one leg ended abruptly just above the knee.

Hartley was breathing slowly and deeply with a hideous bubbling sound, and every now and again he coughed feebly and blood seeped from the corner of his mouth. The parson seemed quite unaware, his eyes on the breviary in his hands. Suddenly Booth groaned and stirred, and the parson put aside his prayer book.

'Are you ready to make your peace now, my son?' the parson's voice asked equably. 'Are you prepared to confess your sins? Tell me the names of your conspirators, or at least,' he amended, seeing the far-away glaze on Booth's eyes, 'at least the names of your leaders.'

Booth moaned and muttered something, and the parson bent his ear to Booth's lips.

114

'Yes?' he said encouragingly. Jess watched the scene as if mesmerised. 'Come now, there is not much time,' the parson went on eagerly. 'Make your peace while there is yet time. Speak, Booth, and tell me.'

Booth stared up at him. Jess saw him struggle to take a breath and make a determined effort to speak.

'Can – you – keep – a – secret?'

The words issued from Booth's mouth as if dragged out with tremendous effort. Jess caught his breath.

'Yes, of course, yes!' Parson Robertson said eagerly. His eyes gleamed with anticipation and he leaned forward anxiously.

Booth closed his eyes. 'So – can – I.'

The words died away on a drifting diminuendo, and Booth's head fell to one side. Jess knew he was gone. The parson opened Booth's eye with a disbelieving finger, and then exclaimed irritably, 'Dammit, he's dead.'

Jess could not remember how he got home to Marsden that day. He was too numb and shocked at John Booth's death. The following day he heard that Sam Hartley had died too. Both men had kept silent to the end.

Mellors' bitter rage about his blighted

115

attempt on the mill was only slightly mollified when he heard Jess's account of Booth's loyalty and death. He stormed up and down the inn parlour, mourning the death of his friends and the injuries of others which had to be kept secret from the authorities lest the group be discovered. He vowed vengeance of the most terrible kind, and exhorted his close friends Walker and Thorpe and Jess to swear death to the enemy with him.

The others, except for Jess, were both grief stricken and anxious to avenge their defeat. But Jess was still too benumbed by the shock of Booth's death to think or react at all to Mellors' vehemence. He watched the young man rave and thought sadly how at one time Mellors' exhortations would have moved him profoundly. But no more. He had seen what Mellors' impetuousness could lead to.

He woke in the grey light of dawn on Monday to find Maggie's thin arms about him and his head resting on her flabby breasts.

'What is it, Jess love?' she asked softly, in a concerned and gentle tone Jess did not remember hearing in months. 'Tha's been weeping like a babby i' thy sleep half o' t' night. Art tha hungry, love?'

Jess drew her closer but she rose from the

bed and went into the kitchen, reappearing with a crust of bread in her hands. 'Here, lovey, take this,' she said. Jess looked at her wonderingly. 'I know, tha's wondering how I could have come by it wi' bread the price it is, but have no fear, I've not stole it. Jenny brought it down from t' big house yesterday. She were right sorry not to see thee,' Maggie explained.

Jess took the crust and bit into it without interest. It was easier to eat than to explain to Maggie that his tears were not of hunger but for a dead, much-loved friend.

'Come back to bed, love. Tha'll catch thy death o' cold,' he invited her softly, but Maggie drew a shawl about her thin shoulders.

'Nay, it's time tha got ready if tha's to be at t' mill by five,' she said stiffly. 'Come on, shake thissen, while I make thee and Maria some gruel,' and she went back into the kitchen.

The next couple of days passed in a guilt-laden haze for Jess. Somehow he felt directly responsible for the death of John Booth. If only he had protested against violence as his instincts had suggested, maybe Booth too, man of peace that he was, would have supported Jess's protests, then perhaps the attack which had led to Booth's death would never have taken place.

Perhaps. Life was full of possibilities and chances, crossroads of choice which never returned in the light of later knowledge. Remorse was useless, Jess knew. Booth could never be resurrected. But maybe if Jess had learnt something from his death, to stand by his conscience instead of allowing himself to be persuaded by men of stronger will than himself, then maybe some good would come of it.

Jess mourned bitterly for Booth. He could not bring himself to go down to the Warreners and face Mellors again for a day or two, for fear that his guilt and sadness should make him cry out against the man he felt was also partly responsible. Instead he sat in his chair by the low fire at home at nights, gazing into the embers and regretting bitterly what might have been. He barely heard Maggie talking to him, but he did look up when she mentioned a word that struck agony into him.

'And I hear tell as them Luddites attacked Cartwright's mill and got some of themselves killed,' she was saying. 'Some of them friends of thine, I reckon. I'm not asking, mind, but I hope as how tha had nowt to do wi' it, Jess, for Mrs Ramsbottom told me as t' magistrates have declared mill-breaking to be a capital offence, and it's hanging for them as they catch who had owt to do wi' t' Rawfolds' business.'

Her lips pursed in a hard line and she went on rocking the baby in her arms. Jess kept silent. How could he tell her about the attack and Booth's death, and let her fear for his safety if she knew? He had brought enough worry to his family without the additional fear that he could be caught and hanged. So he held his tongue.

Josiah Denshaw sat in the comfortably furnished parlour of Justice Radcliffe's house in Milnsbridge. It was warm and cosy by the fire with a glass of hot water and rum in his hands, but he still felt angered by the news.

'So what art tha going to do about it then, Radcliffe? These villains can't be allowed to do such things and get away scot-free, tha knows.'

Radcliffe stretched his legs towards the fire and patted his ample stomach. 'Of course not, Denshaw. I'm putting up a reward for information which could lead to the arrest of the ringleaders.'

'Is that all? Tha doesn't know t' Colne Valley folk if tha thinks that'll be enough to make 'em talk. What art tha doing beside?'

'Well, Hartley is being buried in Halifax tomorrow and with luck we should catch some of the Ludds cutting work to attend. Then there's Booth's funeral at Huddersfield Parish Church on Wednesday and we've another chance then.'

'Aye,' Denshaw rumbled. 'Knowing their loyalty, it's likely they'll want to pay their last respects. We shall have to watch who's missing from t' mills tomorrow.'

'But of course absence from work is no proof of a man's being in league with the Ludds, you follow,' Radcliffe went on. 'Only an indication for us who to watch.'

'But they could get up to more of their devilment if tha doesn't clap hands on 'em soon!'

'Precisely. That is why I'm suggesting that you get some form of protection up at Brackenhurst. Many big houses have already been broken into by the Ludds in search of arms, and you are undoubtedly on their list of millowners to antagonise and put out of business.'

'I've guns and a grown son, and as fierce a wolfhound as any Ludd could wish to meet. If they've any respect for their skins they'll keep well clear o' Brackenhurst and o' my mill.'

'That's what Cartwright thought when he

mounted guards with muskets and a watch-
dog at his mill. And an alarm bell and
carboys of acid to thwart attackers, but he
damn near came to grief despite it. Listen to
me, Denshaw, get the military to put a
guard on your house as well as on the mill.
I'd be afraid to leave Miss Susannah at
home alone if I were you.'

'Aye, 'appen tha's right,' murmured
Denshaw reluctantly. 'Appen I'd best go see
t' captain in charge o' t' Bays.'

So an hour later Denshaw entered the Red
Lion at Marsden, the headquarters of the
King's Bays. John Race, the innkeeper,
recognised him and hastened forward to
serve him, leaving the bunch of roistering,
half-drunken soldiers in the taproom to
wait.

'I want to see t' captain,' said Denshaw.
'What room is he in?'

'Up in my parlour, Mester Denshaw. He's
commandeered it, like. Captain Northcliffe,
his name is.'

'I'll see myself up – get thee back to thy
serving,' said Denshaw and mounted the
stairs.

As he entered Race's parlour he saw a
young man of not more than twenty-five,
with a mop of black hair and his booted feet
propped up on the table.

'Yes?' the young man demanded.

'Captain Northcliffe? I'm Josiah Denshaw.'

The words had a magical effect. All traces of languour left the young man instantly and he leapt to his feet, dragging on his braided jacket at the same time.

'Mr Denshaw — at your service, sir. Forgive my informality, but you caught me unawares. What can I do for you, sir?'

'Don't be so blasted formal, lad. I want your help.' Denshaw's roving gaze was taking in the details of the room, the sword in its scabbard on a chair, the spurs, the cards on the table, and a half-consumed decanter of brandy alongside the glass tumbler. Added to this was the noise rising from the taproom below of shouting, carousing soldiers and their wenches and the stale stench of tobacco and old ale.

'Sir?' The young officer was standing stiffly by a chair, waiting for Denshaw to seat himself and thus allow him to stand at ease.

'Blast thy formality, lad. Like I said, I want thy help, but we can't talk here. I want thee to put a guard on my house, Brackenhurst, but I'd prefer we talked about it in comfort. So come up to t' house tonight — eight o'clock — have dinner wi' us.'

The young man's face lit up. 'I'd be delighted, sir. Thank you very much.' There was no doubting the enthusiasm in his voice. It would be a change for him from this noisy, bawdy place, Denshaw thought. He seemed a likeable, intelligent enough youth. It wasn't often they had company up at the house. It'd be a pleasant change.

'Right then, eight o'clock,' said Denshaw, and left abruptly.

Susannah was lighting the candles on the table and checking that Hannah had indeed put out all the cutlery when the door bell rang. Denshaw saw both Robert and Susannah look up in surprise.

'Who can that be, just at supper time?' Susannah wondered aloud.

Denshaw cleared his throat and put down his paper casually. 'Oh, that'll be t' young officer I asked to come and talk wi' me. Captain Northcliffe. I asked him to have a bite wi' us.'

Susannah threw up her hands in horror. 'Oh, Papa! Couldn't you have warned me?' she remonstrated, and hastened from the room to arrange another place setting. Robert too, Denshaw noticed, sat up with a look of interest on his face.

Hannah ushered Captain Northcliffe into the room. He advanced towards Denshaw

123

with a smile and his hand outstretched.

'Very civil of you to invite me to supper, sir,' he said. 'You can have no idea what it means to a soldier to have a taste of civilisation occasionally.'

'My son, Robert,' Denshaw said, indicating Robert who rose and came graciously to meet Northcliffe and shake hands with him diffidently.

'And my daughter, Susannah.' It gave Denshaw a certain malicious pleasure to see his daughter flush with embarrassment as she entered, having to dispose of the collection of knives and forks in her hand before she could offer it shyly to the officer. Denshaw noticed too how young Northcliffe's eyes lit up at the sight of her pretty flushed face and glossy curls.

Denshaw was delighted with himself that he had surprised both of them, and it made him feel like a puppet master manipulating the strings. And he enjoyed being able to manipulate others.

The evening passed pleasantly, only Robert withdrawing his hesitantly-proffered interest when he realised the officer's attention was wholly ascribed to his sister. Denshaw watched with growing satisfaction the evident liking between the young couple.

'Get her safely married off,' he said to

himself gleefully, 'and then she'll have no mind to meddle wi' my affairs any more. A husband and bairns – that's what she needs to keep her occupied.' And the discovery that the young officer was himself a mill-owner's son from York, a bachelor, and that his father was a manufacturer of wool too, filled Denshaw's cup. What better alliance could he hope for for Sukey, short of Robert's suggestion of a title? No, it all fitted in very well. He beamed genially around the table.

When young Northcliffe left, promising to return on the morrow with a detachment of men to sleep in the stables and guard the house, Denshaw could see he was obviously looking forward to leading the detachment himself, so as to be near the attractive daughter of the house.

And Sukey excused herself and went to bed early, smiling and humming. No reprimand came from her usually outspoken lips about the unexpected guest. Denshaw went to bed happily, congratulating himself on his cleverness. After all, he wasn't renowned as a shrewd and cunning businessman for nothing!

Nine

Sam Hartley's shattered body was laid to rest in Halifax on the following Wednesday, and such a crowd of working folk turned out to pay tribute to his bravery that the mill-owners grew uneasy. It was true that the people walked in silence, but the tokens of mourning that they wore and the heavy, oppressive silence in their ranks that bore evidence to their deep underlying feeling, caused the magistrates to fear a civil outcry against their colleague's cruel death.

Accordingly they decided not to risk a public riot when John Booth's body was to be interred the following day. His funeral was to be in Huddersfield, well known to be the hotbed of Luddite activities in the area, so it was decided to inter Booth's remains secretly at six in the morning instead of at noon.

But soon before noon the market place in Huddersfield began to fill slowly with silent, grey figures huddled inside their coats against the drizzling rain. Jess stood against the wall of the Brown Cow Inn, his collar turned up against the rain and his hair dribbling rivulets of water down his neck.

It seemed odd to be in the town again. He had not been in Huddersfield since the days he used to take his cloth to the Cloth Hall to sell. Little had changed on the surface, however. Old Bradley still had his fish stall in the corner of the market place, the croppers in Nelson's cropping shop opposite were still at their dubbing boards scraping cloth with teazles to raise the pile, and the click-click of the hand-shears in the upper room could still be heard razing the nap. Constable Walton stood at the door of his tobacco shop, puffing with satisfaction on his pipe as though to advertise his wares, and watching the silent throng moving peaceably down Kirkgate towards the Parish Church.

Jess fell in with the crowd, moving quietly along the slippery wet cobblestones, and as he passed the yard of the Pack Horse Inn, Mellors and Thorpe fell in step beside him.

'All these folk,' murmured Mellors, 'and all in their Sunday best too. That just shows how much i' sympathy wi' us the folk of Huddersfield are.'

'More like they have sympathy wi' a chap

who was killed cruelly in t' prime of his life,' retorted Jess without thinking. Mellors regarded him in surprise.

'Dost think it's only Booth they care for?' he asked, his eyebrows high and arched. 'Nay, it's to show they approve o' t' Ludds and what we're doing on their behalf, I'm sure on it.'

Jess kept silent. He hadn't intended to snap at Mellors but somehow he felt disappointed. Mellors hadn't expressed any remorse at Booth's death, only regret that the Rawfolds attack was a failure. Moreover, Jess felt uncomfortable that he had no Sunday best suit to wear as a sign of respect for his dead friend. His one and only suit and a strip of crepe fastened around his arm as a token of his grief was the best he could muster. Mellors and Walker wore their best suits, but Mellors was the stepson of the cropping shop owner.

'We'll walk close to t' hearse, lads,' Mellors was saying to Thorpe, 'and then 'appen at t' graveside I'll get chance to say a few words.'

To stir up the crowd, the thought came swiftly into Jess's head without conscious thought. Mellors wants us to use this tragic occasion to further his own ends! Anger rose furiously inside Jess. Mellors could use men, even his so-called friends, to pursue his intentions without any real thought or concern for them at all. He merely wanted to antagonise the millowners, destroy their business in the name of the common people, yet for one of them, his own close friend, he could not spare a tear or a jot of pity.

Without further deliberation Jess felt all his comradeship and sympathy with this man disappear, submerged without trace as Booth's coffin soon would be. What a guileless fool he had been to follow this man blindly, not listening to or heeding the pricks of his own conscience! For once in his life Jess made an instant decision. He must break with Mellors and all he stood for. It was true the Valley folk were still oppressed and in need of liberation, but Mellors' methods of violence and death were not the right way. Jess did not know what the answer was to their plight, only that Mellors' way was wrong.

He must tell Mellors now that he had finished with the Luddite cause. He turned his head to look at the younger man, but Mellors' brow was furrowed and he was looking anxiously over the heads of the people in front of him.

'There's summat up,' Mellors muttered impatiently. 'People are turning away at t' church gates. What's wrong? What is it?'

The crowd had by now come to a halt at the bottom of Kirkgate, milling slowly outside the churchyard walls. Mellors pushed his way through towards the front, and met a couple of men who were returning.

'What's amiss?' Mellors demanded of them. 'Aren't we to be allowed in then? Do they think to ban us from t' funeral of a friend?'

'Nay, we're too late, they tell us,' answered one of the men, his grizzled hair and bushy eyebrows bespattered with raindrops. 'Booth were buried at six this morning, seemingly.'

Disappointed murmurs rippled through the crowd as the news spread rapidly. Mellors' face flushed with anger.

'They've cheated us!' he cried, grabbing Jess's arm in his vexation. 'They've deliberately buried him unbeknownst to us all so as to cheat us! But I'll not be thwarted so easily, damn 'em, that I won't.'

'What'll tha do, George?' asked Thorpe anxiously. Jess could see he was concerned about the noise Mellors was making in the street. Curious passers-by, having naught else now to engage their attention, were stopping to listen.

'Cartwright! He's the man responsible – I'll get him! We'll do for him!' cried Mellors.

'Sithee now, lad, tha'rt overwrought,' muttered Thorpe soothingly. 'Come up to t' Pack Horse for a glass of ale wi' me. Tha'll come too, Jess?'

Thorpe took Mellors' arm and persuaded him to move off, reluctantly, up Kirkgate. Mellors was still red-faced and his eyes flashed fire as he swore vengeance on Cartwright and Denshaw and all evil-mongering millowners.

'Hush now, tha'll say too much,' snapped Thorpe. 'Tha'll be t' death of us all, the way tha going on.'

They reached the cobbled yard of the Pack Horse Inn, and had to pause to let a carriage rumble slowly by. Mellors started forward, his eyes bulging, when he saw its portly occupant.

'Denshaw, blast his soul.' he muttered, and would have sprung for the door of the carriage if Thorpe had not restrained him. 'Denshaw, just finished eating a fine, hearty meal wi' Radcliffe or some other of his fine friends, no doubt! But I'll get him, I swear, or my name's not George Mellors! I'll watch him bleed like Booth and enjoy watching him die!'

Thorpe jerked him towards the inn door. 'Come on,' he said roughly. 'Tha coming too, Jess?'

Jess hesitated. 'No. I'm going home.'

Mellors turned. 'Tha's time for a glass wi' us afore we walk back, lad. There's matters to discuss.'

'No.'

The redness left Mellors' face. 'Na look, lad, there's no need to take on so. I feel as disappointed as thee over t' funeral, but we'll get us own back on t' devils. Come in and we'll talk it over.'

Jess straightened and looked him straight in the eyes, then took a deep breath. 'I'm not coming. And I'll not be at t' Warreners neither. I've done wi' t' Luddites.'

Mellors and Thorpe stared at him uncomprehendingly. Mellors' voice took on a very reasoned tone.

'Sithee Jess, I've told thee, we're all upset but that's not t' end on it, I promise thee. I know how fond tha was of Booth – we all were – but just like Denshaw has sworn to wade i' our blood, I'll swear we'll wade i' his.'

'That's just it,' said Jess quietly, 'I'm having nowt more to do wi' blood and death. I've finished, like I said. I'm no more a Ludd. That's all there is to it.'

He turned to go. There, now it was said, and he was surprised at his own outspokenness. There was no further point in discussing it. He'd finished with them and he'd told them. That was the end of it.

Mellors grabbed his arm. His eyes were feverish as they bored into Jess's. 'Tha swore an oath,' he reminded him.

'I know.' In fact that was what troubled Jess most. But if he remembered rightly, it did not say in the oath that he could never stop being a Ludd, only that he could never speak of what he knew, and as he would never dream of betraying them it did not seem irrevocable.

'The oath of secrecy,' Mellors reminded him.

'Aye.'

'Think again, lad. Tha knows we mun get rid of t' oppressors.'

'Not this way, it's wrong. I've done wi' it.'

'Very well then.' Mellors' voice was cold and bitter. 'We've no room for cowards. Be off wi' thee then, Jess Drake, but think on that one word out o' place'll mean thy death.'

Jess could see Thorpe's wide eyes over Mellors' shoulder. He was nodding his head, and there was fright in his eyes.

'I know, and I'll never betray thee,' Jess said quietly. 'But I want nowt to do wi' thee – ever,' and this time when he turned to go no hand restrained him. His quiet tone of conviction surprised even himself; it was not like him usually to be so emphatic, but he meant what he said, and Mellors knew it.

It was late afternoon by the time Jess reached Marsden again. He did not want to return home too early or he would have to render account to Maggie, who believed him to be at the mill as usual. Instead he loitered on the road and turned off into Dungeon Wood so as to gain shelter from the ever-drizzling rain.

An overturned tree trunk afforded him a seat and Jess sat hugging his knees and thinking over what he had done. For once in his life he had made an instantaneous decision and acted upon it. He was glad of it, relieved of his responsibility any longer to join in with Mellors' violent plans. His conscience was slightly assuaged that he had made the right choice, but it still bled for Booth's death. Booth too had sensed that the Luddites' actions were not wholly justifiable, and the price he paid for stifling his conscience had been death. By rights Jess should have died too.

Jess's tears scalded his cheeks despite the rain as he mourned his friend in the privacy of Dungeon Wood. When the tears abated Jess looked up at the arching trees above him, and thought how he used to climb into those branches in his youth. This wood had been the confidant of most of his heart's woes over the years, right from the time he was a lad and used to run here to weep in private anger and frustration after his father had whipped him for some childish misdemeanour. It was here he had wept for his dead mother the tears that he could not show to the rest of the world. It was here that he stood as a youth, panting and eager for his lovely Maggie, and parted from her sadly as the moon rose. Indeed, there were few of Jess's secrets the wood did not know.

Clogshod feet on the roadway below roused him. The millworkers were going home so it was safe for him to return to his cottage now without fear of questioning from Maggie. He rose, stretched his stiff limbs, shook the rain out of his hair and set off up the moor.

Maggie was slumped in a chair, her eyes closed. She opened her eyes when he came in, looked at him vacantly, then rose slowly and began pottering about the little kitchen. No questions came from her lips. She appeared totally uninterested in the world about her.

The door opened and Maria breezed in, took off her shawl and started looking about for something to eat. Jess noticed something

135

unusual about her movements, could not place what it was at first, then realised she was moving with unaccustomed stiffness. He thought despairingly that she must be going lame, as loom tenders often did from standing all day, and then saw to his amazement that she had shoes on her feet and was moving awkwardly because she was unused to wearing them.

He pointed at her feet. 'Where did tha come by them?' he asked. Maggie's gaze followed his finger and she stood mouth agape for a moment, then lost interest. Maria went on stirring the contents of the pot over the fire without answering.

'Did tha hear me? Where'd them shoes come from?' he asked again. Maria straightened and looked at him without replying. There was a proud, defiant look in her eyes. 'Well then? Tha couldn't a bought 'em,' Jess went on.

'No, I didn't.'

'Well then?'

'Well then what?'

Jess sighed patiently. 'Did someone give 'em thee?'

'Of course. Tha doesn't think I stole 'em, dost tha?'

'There's no call for thy lip, lass,' Jess remonstrated quietly. 'Who gave 'em thee?'

'Mester Briggs, if tha must know.'

There was a silence so tangible in the little kitchen that Jess felt he could almost take hold of it in his hands. Undoubtedly the same thoughts were going through Maggie's head as through his own, but she kept silent. Either she didn't care, or she was leaving Jess to cope with this situation, and after the tumult of emotion he had so recently endured, Jess felt he could face no more discord. Still, he could not leave matters thus.

'Why did he give 'em thee?'

Maria shrugged her shoulders. 'Why not? They're not new. Mrs Briggs has no more use for 'em, being bedfast, so he gave 'em me.'

'But why thee, out of all t' lasses in t' mill?'

'Maybe 'cos I'm t' prettiest, who knows?' She was trying to pass it off with a flippant joke, but Jess knew her too well to be taken in by it.

'What hast tha done for him that he should favour thee?'

The words were quietly spoken but they had the effect of a thunderbolt in the room. Maggie and Maria both stared at him wide-eyed.

'What art tha suggesting, Jess?' It was Maggie's voice.

'She knows. Now answer me, Maria.'

137

Maria jutted her hip defiantly and tossed her head. 'I know how to take care of meself,' she snapped. 'I know I can get favours out of Briggs by being – nice – to him. How else would I get food enough to eat and shoes for me feet? Tha cannot provide food enough for us, let alone shoes, so I mun do what I can for meself.'

Jess saw Maggie move away into the corner. She was tacitly admitting agreement with Maria by not scolding her in alliance with him. He felt defeated. It was true, he could not provide for his family, but it hurt to be taunted with it.

'So tha thinks to fend for thyself – by selling him thy body,' he murmured.

Maria rounded on him. 'I do not sell – I give! And what I give is my own to give, not thine nor anyone else's.' Her voice was high and near to hysteria. 'And I can fend for meself. Don't fear I shall bring thee home a bastard to care for. I'm not stupid! I know what I'm doing, which is more than can be said for thee!'

Jess heard the bedroom door close quietly. Maggie had slunk away to hide, to avoid joining the battle. For the first time he could remember, his faithful ally had let him down. Jess sat dejectedly on a chair and looked at Maria.

'Make of it what tha can,' said Maria proudly, 'but I eat well and my limbs are straight as a result. I don't get cracked over t' head wi' a billy roller nor whipped neither. Seems plain commonsense to me. And that's the way I'm going to go on, so there.'

Jess hung his head. What reason was there to argue? The girl was right, she was better able to look after herself than he was, so who was he to argue with her methods?

Abigail came in and ran to him, flinging her soft arms about his neck. 'Oh, tha'rt soaking!' she cried, feeling his sodden jacket, then flung her arms about him again. But even the love of his favourite child could not alleviate Jess Drake's mental anguish that night.

Ten

Josiah Denshaw watched his daughter laying the table and approved the sight. She was a pretty wench, there was no doubt of it. Her eyes shone with the sparkle they always did at about this time of day. He looked at the clock on the mantelshelf. A quarter before eight.

Captain Northcliffe would be here soon. That accounted for Sukey's sparkle and her light, tripping footsteps as she hastened to the kitchen and back again. Ever since Denshaw had asked Northcliffe to put a guard on the house, Susannah had insisted that Northcliffe should dine with them.

'After all, Papa, it wouldn't be fitting for a cavalry officer to have to eat at the kitchen table with his men!' she had exclaimed, wide-eyed at the thought of such impropriety, but Denshaw had not been taken in by her guileless, innocent air. He knew his scheming daughter too well. But he had simply agreed, reluctantly on the surface, but inwardly delighted with his plan.

Now the young couple had reached the stage of addressing each other by their Christian names instead of Captain Northcliffe and Miss Susannah. It gladdened Denshaw's heart every time he heard Sukey say 'Charles' in that wondering, caressing tone she could use on occasion.

Denshaw watched her rearrange the flowers in the copper bowl on the table for the fourth time.

'I thowt tha'd gotten a maid?' he growled from the depths of his easy chair. 'Seems to me tha's doing all t' running about thissen 'stead o' leaving it to her. Why can't she lay t' table and such like?'

Susannah coloured. 'Jenny, you mean? Oh yes, she's a nice enough little creature but terribly shy, Papa, you've no idea. She's terrified of coming into the rooms where "the gentry" are, as she puts it, and nothing on earth would induce her to answer a ring at the front door. She's just too shy and,' Susannah added in a lowered tone, 'to tell the truth, I think she's a little bit well, slow on the uptake, as one might say.'

'Daft, is she?' Denshaw asked. Susannah laid her finger on her lips.

'Hush Papa, she might hear you.'

'Well where's t' sense in paying a maid who does nowt, that's what I'd like to know?'

'Oh, she works very well in the kitchen, Papa, and doing the cleaning, the brasses and everything. She just prefers to stay out of sight, and frankly I think it's better that way.'

The doorbell rang. Susannah started and Denshaw was gratified to see the flush start to spread up from her neck and across her cheeks.

'The captain's here,' she said, and darted from the room. No doubt to have a couple of minutes in private with the young officer in the hallway, reflected Denshaw. He saw that Robert was smiling lazily too, as if the same thought was crossing his mind.

At the supper table Susannah sat between her brother and Captain Northcliffe and Denshaw sat opposite her. She looked quite delectable in the candlelight, her father thought, her glossy ringlets falling on bare white shoulders, and the pink glow of her cheeks added to the green lustre of her gown giving her the appearance of a ripe and luscious russet apple. Fruit ripe for the picking, he thought, and looked at the young officer. His air of rapt attention as he gazed at her undoubtedly meant he thought so too. Denshaw was very happy with the way his plan was going.

The conversation inevitably turned to the reason for the captain's presence. Robert enquired idly what the Luddites' latest manoeuvres had been.

'They're lying low at the moment, it seems, after their failure at Rawfolds,' Captain Northcliffe replied.

Denshaw snorted. 'That fool Cartwright! He thought he'd got his mill properly defended, but I know better. Cannon's what he needs.'

'He did succeed in staving them off, sir,' Northcliffe pointed out.

'Staving 'em off is not enough! They want teaching a damn good lesson, one as they won't forget too easily,' Denshaw roared.

Northcliffe lowered his gaze to the empty plate before him. 'Two men died as a result of that attack,' he said quietly.

'Serves 'em right, the ungrateful fools! If they'd stayed at their jobs and carried on working, peaceful-like, it'd never have happened.'

Northcliffe made no reply. Susannah was watching his expression thoughtfully.

'You do not seem to care for your mission, Charles,' she said softly. 'Does quelling Luddite riots not meet with your approval?'

Northcliffe looked up at her. 'They are my orders, and I cannot refuse,' he replied, 'but it is not an assignment to my liking. I do not care to fire on unarmed men. Give me a detachment of Frenchmen to fight, armed with muskets and sabres as we are, and the fight is fair. But this,' he shrugged and looked down at his plate again.

'What's this? What's this?' Denshaw demanded. 'An officer trained to obey, and yet questioning his orders? What is the world coming to?'

Northcliffe looked him straight in the eyes. 'I know a man, a private in Huddersfield, who refused to fire on an unarmed

143

Luddite at Rawfolds the other day. He too had principles. Do you know what punishment his officers have deemed fit to impose on that man? Three hundred lashes of the whip.'

Denshaw heard Susannah's gasp of horror. True, it did seem a disproportionate punishment, but then the man had disobeyed orders. The world could only exist by those in authority giving orders, and the lower ranks obeying those orders implicitly. He said so to Northcliffe.

'And do you feel, sir, that a man should carry out orders even if he feels them to be wrong? To be against the code of human conduct?'

'No common man has the right – or the ability – to think!' Denshaw shouted. 'That's t' way t' world is arranged. We wi' brains think and plan – and give orders. T' rest does as they're told. I'm sorry for t' man, but he disobeyed, so whipping is t' only course for him.'

'Even if he dies for his convictions?' murmured Northcliffe.

'Aye, well, if he wants to make a martyr of hisself, that's his look-out,' countered Denshaw. 'If he'd thowt first, 'appen he'd a done as he were told.'

Northcliffe glanced at the clock. 'Well, if

you would be so kind as to excuse me, it's time I took my patrol up to the mill and Valeside,' he said, and rose and pushed back his chair. 'That was an excellent supper, Susannah. Thank you very much for your kindness.'

Susannah blushed again. 'I'll see you out, Charles,' she said, and they left the room together.

Next day Captain Northcliffe reappeared much earlier than he was expected. Susannah was in a flurry of excitement when she brought him into the parlour.

'Papa, Charles has something of importance he wishes to discuss with you,' she said, and flashing Charles a warm smile, left the two men alone together.

'What is it then, lad?' Denshaw demanded.

The young officer appeared very agitated. 'I said yesterday that it appeared the Ludds were lying low for a time. I was mistaken. A group of them calling themselves the Avengers, made an attempt on Cartwright's life yesterday.'

Denshaw jerked upright in his char. 'Cartwright? Is he dead then?'

'No, but it was his good luck that he was not killed.'

'What happened?'

'They must have known about the military hearing in Huddersfield yesterday afternoon, and that Cartwright was to give evidence about the attack on his mill and the soldier who refused to fire.'

'Oh aye, him,' Denshaw said, remembering his outburst the previous night. 'Well?'

'Well, after Cartwright had left the hearing, he took his horse and rode out of Huddersfield. About a mile out of town they were waiting for him, in Bradley Wood. They fired two shots at him, missing him by a hairs-breadth. Fortunately his horse took fright and bolted so they didn't catch up with him to make a further attempt.'

'In broad daylight, eh?' mused Denshaw. 'By God, they've got murderous intentions, this lot. And your soldiers refused to fire on a bunch of would-be murderers like that, eh?'

'Well, that's a matter I've not come to discuss, Mr Denshaw. I'm concerned for your safety.'

'For my safety?' Denshaw exploded. 'They'll not dare try to do owt to me!'

'I wouldn't be so certain, sir. You, as a mill-owner, stand in as great danger as Cartwright, and I should not be at all surprised if they make some attempt on your life.'

'I can take care of mesen,' roared Den-

146

shaw.

'Possibly sir, but I should like to ensure it. I can offer you a guard to accompany you wherever you go.'

'A guard? Like a babby being taken out by his wet-nurse? What dosta take me for, lad? Some snivelling cowardly fellow, is it? I've me pistol and a fast horse, and I've cannon up at t' mill. That's all t' defence I need, lad, and that's all I'm having!'

Northcliffe looked at the floor uncomfortably. Denshaw softened a little. 'Not that I'm not grateful, like, for thy concern, but I'm not having any. So that's that. Wilt have a glass o' brandy wi' me afore tha goes?'

Captain Northcliffe declined. Denshaw watched him through the window riding off down the gravel drive with his men. Likeable young chap, Denshaw thought, but he'd have to learn, like everyone else, that no one dictated to Josiah Denshaw.

It was two days later when Jess, no longer able to frequent the Warreners, was sitting alone in the taproom of the Red Lion. He knew it was the soldiers' haunt, but his conscience was clear enough now. He no longer had aught to do with the Luddites. The only qualm of guilt that remained with him was over John Booth's death. Every day in the mill the machines seemed to be taunting him with their never-ending clack of accusation. 'Booth's dead, Booth's dead, your fault, your fault,' they seemed to be saying, and Jess was glad to escape the sound and drown the thought in a tankard of ale.

He sat now in a corner, out of the lantern light and unaware of the soldiers' banter. But then he became aware that the tone of their conversation had changed on the entrance of one of their comrades. This young soldier flung himself moodily in a chair and refused the ale they offered him, and Jess could hear their kindly words of consolation.

'Cheer up, Jack, lad, he'll pull through,' one of them was saying. 'He's a sturdy lad, he'll survive.'

Yet another man with the worry of ailing children, Jess wondered. He looked somewhat young to be married and a father yet though.

Another soldier entered. A look of surprise crossed his ruddy, weatherbeaten face. 'What, no carousing tonight lads? Where's the lasses? Why art tha all looking so glum, eh?' he demanded heartily. The sullen soldier looked at him resentfully.

'Hush,' said the third, 'Jack's brother got flogged today for refusing to fire on a Luddite.'

'Oh aye, I heard,' said the ruddy youth. 'Three hundred lashes, weren't it? How'd he go on?'

Angry growls came from the sullen youth by the fire. 'They had to stop it,' the other interrupted before he could erupt. 'After twenty lashes he were in a bad way, all bleeding and only half conscious. Mester Cartwright were there, and he asked t' officer to stop. But t' officer were for going on. After five more lashes the crowd got angry and started shouting, so t' officer called a stop to it.'

'But not before he made a hell of a mess of our Joseph!' the angry youth cried. 'Tha should a seen him – blood pouring from his back, he looked like a carcase just out o' t' abattoir! God knows if he'll ever recover!'

The youth's face was twisted and compressed, and Jess could see it was only with great effort that he was preventing himself from weeping. No wonder, thought Jess, having to see his brother treated so inhumanely.

His friend patted him reassuringly on the shoulder. 'He'll recover, never fear, Jack. He's a hardy lad, is thy Joseph.'

'I'll murder the bastards who did it, if I get half a chance,' the youth muttered.

'Nay lad,' said the ruddy one. 'Murder the Luddites instead when tha's ordered, like thy brother should a done. Them's the devils causing all t' trouble. I wish I knew who their General Ludd were – I'd shoot him without a moment's hesitation.'

Jess shrank back into the corner, fearing lest they might turn and ask him what he knew. For the Luddite secrets he carried must go with him to the grave, he knew, or his life would be forfeit.

He drank up and left the Red Lion as quickly and inconspicuously as he could. Was there no end to this inhumanity, he wondered as he walked home. Overseers flogging children, Luddites fighting mill-owners, and now soldiers whipped because of Luddite activities, as well as the Ludds' own losses. He was only glad that he had withdrawn from the group and no longer had any part in whatever Mellors might plan next. With luck the Luddites would recognise the Rawfolds' business as their death knell and leave matters alone, for a short time at least. Maybe others like himself had been shocked by the bloodshed that night and had withdrawn their allegiance as he had done. And in that case, maybe Mellors had seen the danger signal and would call off any further plans for violence. It was an optimistic thought, Jess knew, but what else was there if one did not hope?

It was not till next day at the mill that he heard of the Avengers' attempt on Cartwright's life. Jess sighed. So Mellors was not giving up after all. The man was possessed with the idea of vengeance, no matter what the cost. Jess could not help the sinking feeling in his heart. More evil was yet to come, of that he felt sure, and there was nothing he could do to prevent it.

Eleven

Robert tossed aside the *Mercury* irritably and stretched his legs towards the fire. God but he was bored! The newspaper was full of nothing more interesting than Wellington's forays in Spain and the Home Secretary's pronouncements about matters which concerned Robert not a jot. He yawned and stretched his arms above his head.

The coals in the hearth settled with a

crash that half awoke him from his reverie. The fire needed mending, as Hannah would say. But Hannah had the evening off. He remembered seeing her dumpy little figure waddling off down the drive as he stood in the bay window surveying the dismal view. There was no one to talk to at all. Not that Father ever spoke to him; his only conversation was a one-sided diatribe on the rights of millowners and the iniquities of mill-workers. Father did not want to hear of any of the matters which interested Robert, such as cards and horse-riding and betting and pretty women. The mere mention of London made the old man's expression tighten and he refused to discuss it.

And Susannah. She was passably intelligent for a sister, he supposed, or she had been until recently. Now she and that young Northcliffe spent all their time gazing at each other with love-lorn expressions and soulful sighs. Down-right nauseating it was to watch. Anyway Susannah, like Father, was out for the evening, visiting friends she had said, but possibly that was only to conceal a secret meeting with her beau.

What a bore life was! It had been an infernal bore ever since he'd been exiled here in Yorkshire, away from the gaiety and excitement of London and his friends. Blast

Father, recalling him just as his luck appeared to be turning at last, and he was on the verge of being introduced to the Prince Regent's circle. By now he could have been well established in the gay, fast crowd who set the trends in London and Brighton. If only Father had not cut off his allowance at such a crucial time!

What was there for a fellow here in this blasted, barren place if he wasn't to go out of his mind with the sheer monotony of it all? Father was really a remarkably unimaginative man to think a fellow brought up as he was could adapt himself to the tradesman life his father led. It was a mean, blackmailing gesture on his part to deprive Robert of his allowance and force him to live in hermit-like seclusion in such a godforsaken spot. The old man no doubt hoped to steer his interest into the running of the mill, but it was a vain hope. Robert's only interest in it was the money it produced, and if Father was not willing to share the proceeds with him now, then he would have to wait, albeit with impatience. Father was nearing sixty, and although the Denshaws were renowned for their longevity, the time must surely come when Robert would acquire his father's hard-won money.

And when he did succeed to the estate,

Robert promised himself he would not waste his life grubbing around in squalor as his father had done. Not he. He would employ the money to live as a gentleman should. In London, of course, not Yorkshire.

It was growing cold in the parlour. Robert debated whether to go and fetch more coal himself or to have another glass of brandy to warm himself. He decided on the brandy and poured himself a liberal quantity into a tumbler.

If only there was something to do to relieve this boredom! He tossed off the brandy. If only there were another of his own kind with whom he could pass a pleasant evening now and again, to go hunting or have a game of cards, then it wouldn't be so bad. Or some pretty filly with whom he could dally in the flirtatious fashion of the London ladies. Even a more earthy dalliance would suffice, he reflected thinking of the pretty wench who had served him in the Red Lion earlier in the day, with her country-fresh skin and teasing eyes. He could use her for a pleasant hour if only she were in reach.

He was just pouring himself another helping of brandy when a faint noise from a distant part of the house made Robert forget his daydream and sit up with a jerk.

The wolfhound before the fire did not stir.

'Tarquin?' Robert murmured questioningly. The wolfhound raised its head. 'Listen, Tarquin.' The hound twitched its ears, looked enquiringly at its master, and lay down again.

Robert heard the distant sound again, a harsh, scraping noise. Could it be a bolt being drawn? The house was empty save for himself. Robert remembered Captain Northcliffe's warnings about the Luddites' marauding the larger houses in search of weapons. Or they could even be after his father's blood, in view of the many threats he had voiced loudly against the Ludds. The hair at the back of his neck prickled.

'Here, Tarquin,' Robert said softly. The wolfhound padded to his side and sat, still and attentive. He evidently suspected no intruder. But what else could the sound be?

Robert crossed to the door, his hand on the wolfhound's collar, then crept down the corridor towards the back of the house. The prickling crept across his scalp, and Robert cursed himself for a cowardly fool. Near the kitchen door he stumbled over the dog, and swore silently. Then the sound came again – this time loud and clear. It was the harsh, strident coughing of someone in the kitchen.

Robert flung the door wide and stood with his hand on Tarquin's collar, fearful of what he might see. But all he saw was a pale-haired girl sitting warming her hands by the fire. At his abrupt entrance she leapt to her feet and shrank against the far wall, wide-eyed with terror.

Now he remembered. It was that little maid Susannah had taken on some weeks ago, the one she said was too timid to venture out of the kitchen. Jenny, that was her name. He had almost forgotten her existence. He remembered seeing her when she was first taken on, a thin, gawky sick-looking creature she'd been then, but now regular meals had wrought a change in her. Her gleaming fair hair, fire-reddened cheeks and mute, wide eyes gave her an infinitely appealing look.

Robert remembered his dignity as son of the house, and pulled himself together. 'Now then, Jenny, what are you up to?' He spoke loudly to convince himself that his lately felt fear was nothing more than a momentary, insignificant failing. Jenny became more agitated and cowered against the wall, staring at him and the dog.

'Don't get in a state, child, I'll not harm you,' he reassured her, moving forward, but she whimpered and pointed in terror at the

156

hound. 'Oh, it's Tarquin who frightens you, is it? He'll not touch you. Look, I'll send him away.'

Robert pointed to the door. 'Tarquin, out!' The dog lumbered out obediently and Robert closed the door behind him and turned back to Jenny. He saw her eyes begin to fill with tears and her shoulders were trembling, and he felt his manhood begin to stir within him.

By God, he thought, a few weeks at Brackenhurst had certainly improved her! Her thinness still remained, but it was no longer scrawny and starved-looking, but a trim slenderness that appealed to him. Her small young breasts bulged against the thin cloth of her gown as she stood still pressed against the wall. Her long fair hair glistened with gold and red lights in the firelight. Her huge eyes stared at him with the mute, pathetic appeal of a wounded animal.

'Come now, Jenny, don't stand there as if dumbstruck,' he said to her. 'Go fetch me some more coal for the parlour there's a good lass.'

Jenny moved forward slowly and stood waiting hesitantly for him to step aside so that she could pass. He did not move. She looked up at him questioningly.

'Are you still affrighted, Jenny?' he asked

157

her. She did not answer, but simply lowered her gaze and began pleating her skirt nervously with her fingers. Robert slid his arms about her waist and felt her tremble violently. 'You're not frightened of me, are you?' he asked coaxingly.

Jenny shook like a leaf in his arms. 'I do not know thee, sir,' she stammered. It was true. In all the time she had been there he had never spoken to the child. The most he had ever seen of her had been a flickering grey shadow flitting out of sight at his approach.

Then it was time they improved their acquaintance, he decided. It was a pleasant feeling, to hold a little frightened creature in his power thus. It suddenly recalled his youth, when he would find a fallen fledgling sparrow and torment its life away with great delight, until the little thing would expire from terror in his hands. The feeling of power and supremacy was pleasing to one's self-esteem.

'Let me pass sir.' The words were but a whisper, and she fluttered in his arms just like the sparrow chick. He was going to enjoy playing with her, tormenting her until she learned to be more pliant with the master's son. After all, in London many finer wenches than Jenny would be gratified to receive his attentions thus. But he might as well pass a vacant hour with her instead of alone, and moreover the dalliance might help him forget his recent shameful fear that she had occasioned by her coughing.

'No haste, child,' he murmured in her ear. 'Come, give me a kiss.' She turned her head away and he felt her hair brush his cheek. The sensation gave rise to other, stronger sensations and Robert gripped her firmly.

'No, please don't, Master Robert,' she cried, and struggled to free herself from his grasp. He gripped her even more tightly and heard her gasp as he squeezed the breath from her thin body. He forced his mouth down on to hers and kissed her hard and savagely, revelling in her squirming and struggling that roused him even further.

He forced her into the middle of the kitchen and she gave strangled little screams that frightened him. He began to panic. He must stop her making a noise! No one was within hearing, but who knew when Father or Susannah might return? He pressed a hand over Jenny's mouth and dragged her to the floor. Her thin body collapsed under him without too much effort on his part.

Kissing her hard to stop her mouth, he tore at her clothing till it hung in shreds. Jenny lay stiff with terror under him.

Feverish with desire and fright, Robert went on acting without conscious thought until a terrified scream broke from Jenny's lips. He ignored it, engulfed as he was in all-consuming passion. It was a hideous sound she made, a piercing animal sound of sheer terror, like a rabbit tortured in a trap.

Consciousness returned to Robert. He flung himself off the girl and sat up. She lay there still, and hardly seemed to be breathing. Shame and fear flooded Robert. What on earth had he done? She was starting to moan. Robert rose and stumbled to the door, then paused.

Why should he run from the scene like some scared village oaf? Why should he feel humiliated and ashamed? Was he not Robert Denshaw, the master's son, and she only a pauper wench? Why need he fear her?

He knew he had seduced her with as little finesse as a stampeding elephant, but why should she care? Many a maidservant, he knew for a fact, considered it a great honour to be covered by a gentleman instead of by one of their own menial sort. She should be grateful to him for condescending to grant her his attentions, however fleeting. He could not run away. He must stay and show her how she had been honoured. That way he would at least redeem himself in his own

160

eyes as behaving like a man of the world.

He fumbled in his pockets and pulled out a number of small coins. Jenny was rising slowly to her feet, clutching her torn bodice about her and sobbing quietly.

'Here, Jenny, take this,' he said, holding out the coins to her. 'Buy yourself another gown. Straighten your hair now and wash your face, and we'll mention no word of this to anyone, will we?' He smiled a stiff, forced smile, intended to convey both reassurance and his own confidence, but it felt twisted and unconvincing. She did not take the money. Instead, her fair head bent low, she made to slide past him as if she had not heard him. 'Jenny!'

She turned at the sound of his cry, and her eyes were vacant. Robert shuddered. The repelling thought occurred to him that maybe he had just raped an imbecile, seeing those haunted, staring eyes. Susannah had said she was rather slow-witted, now he came to think of it. He felt rather sick.

'Jenny,' he began again awkwardly, then drew himself up and put the money back in his pocket. 'Your position here will be quite safe, I assure you, as long as you remember to do as you are told, and keep your counsel. No one will harm you. You understand me?'

The eyes stared dully at him.

'You must remember to speak of this to no one. Is that clear?'

The girl nodded.

'Good. Now go and fetch the coal.'

She slunk past him. Robert watched her retreating figure and wondered how on earth he could have been so stupid as to waste his time on such an idiotic child. This was one conquest he would never be proud to boast of in the London salons once he returned there.

Boredom, that was the sole cause of this pointless little peccadillo. It was all Father's fault. God! The sooner he could make Father see reason enough to let him return to London and sanity the better!

Robert returned angrily to the parlour and poured himself another generous helping of brandy.

Despite his exhaustion by the time he had finished the day's work and tramped home across the moor, Jess Drake could not sleep. His conscience was easier, it was true, since he had forsworn his allegiance to the Ludds, but he still feared what train of events their earlier actions might have set in motion.

At the moment, naught appeared to be happening since they had failed to kill

Cartwright, but the seeming calm that lay over the valley had a hidden menace in it, like the ominous lull before a violent storm. Jess could not lie easy in his bed. What was it that troubled him?

Maggie still ailed after little Seth's birth, but she struggled gamely on. Abigail still played, happy as a cricket, on the hearth of her own home, and as far as he knew, Jenny was thriving in her God-given new position. Maria nagged his conscience, disappearing nightly without explanation, but her defiant manner pointed to yet another assignation with Briggs.

No, it was something other than his family that vexed his mind. Somehow he knew, as if he had seen or heard it somewhere, that whatever was about to befall would bring grief and hardship with it.

It was uncanny, but Jess could feel the impending tragedy as surely as if it had already occurred, and he was saddened that there was no way in which he could foresce or forestall it. He simply lay sleepless in his bed and fretted.

Twelve

The rainy, depressing days at last changed suddenly with typical April fickleness to gentle sunshine. But the warm peace that lay over the valley had not strength enough to counter the black sullenness in George Mellors' heart.

He strode down the lane leading to Longroyd Bridge and his stepfather's cropping shop feeling the bitterness and anger coursing through his veins so feverishly that it seemed almost that it would burst out from his throbbing temples. Nothing but setbacks and failure had met his determined efforts to drag those blasted capitalists to their knees.

And he was losing his power over his men. He could sense that they no longer followed his lead blindly and trustingly as they once had done. He could even pinpoint the moment when his hitherto unchallenged leadership had begun to wane. It was the night at Rawfolds. Ever since he had been

164

obliged to leave Booth in the enemy's hands, and Booth had died, their trust in him had begun to fade. He knew it, but what else could he have done?

It was a pity about Booth. He had been a worthwhile convert to the cause, with his scholarly, gentle air that betokened breeding and intelligence. They didn't have many of his calibre. His presence at their meetings had lent an air of prestige and integrity to their actions that no mere weaver or cropper could bring. It was a pity about Hartley dying too, of course, but he hadn't quite the same air of intangible authority that Booth had.

Mellors kicked at a pebble angrily. He had hoped their deaths, met so bravely and in silence, would have been regarded as martyrdom and the Ludds as a result would have become even more united. He had even tried to urge this point at meetings, but in some indefinable way their deaths seemed to have had the contrary effect. One after another several members had failed to turn up at meetings; others had quickly found excellent reasons why they could not partake in subsequent Ludd activities, and Mellors could feel his authority over them slipping away uncontrollably like sand through one's fingers.

The throbbing in his temples started again. Everything was going wrong. He must regain control before it was too late. It was up to him, as General Ludd of the area, to collect together his depleting army before its morale sank too low. They must take some form of outstanding action, and that very soon, or they were lost!

But what action? Mellors did not have to consider long. All his anger and frustration were directed at the millowners and with particular venom at Josiah Denshaw as the most irksome of their breed. The man had openly flouted and defied the Ludds, and what was worse, had mocked and jeered at their futile attempts. He must be silenced before he could undo them completely. Of that there was not the slightest flicker of doubt in Mellors' mind, Denshaw must be silenced – for ever.

As he passed the door of a low, whitewashed cottage, Mellors saw a couple of mangy mongrels tearing savagely at the steaming entrails of a pig that the housewife had just thrown out into the yard. Mellors watched in fascination as the dogs growled and pulled hungrily, the yards of guts spreading bloodily across the cobbles. He watched in envy. If only those were Denshaw's guts spattered on the ground for starving curs to devour! He would willingly tear out Denshaw's innards himself and throw them to the dogs, his heart crying out in satisfied vengeance.

And what was more, he would. He could feel a warm glow as he relished the prospect of watching Denshaw die, wallowing in his own blood as he had sworn he would do in the Ludds'.

Mellors' yearning for immediate action rose unbridled. He kicked again at a pebble, as hard as he could, and laughed as it narrowly sped past the white bitch's ear, causing her to drop the booty in her mouth, lay back her ears and growl at him briefly with bared teeth, before snatching up her prize again and slinking away behind the cottage.

He reached his stepfather's yard and turned into the cropping shed, nodding curtly to Smith and Walker who were already busy, sweeping the shears over the cloth in broad, even strokes.

'Morning, lads, morning,' he said, and went straight through the shed into the office beyond. Stepfather was not in. Of course, Mellors remembered now he'd be in Huddersfield on business most of the day as it was market day. Good, that gave Mellors time to think out a detailed plan for the murder of a man like Denshaw was not a matter to be undertaken lightly. It must be carefully planned so that nothing misfired.

Misfired. Pistols. Yes, shooting might be a good course, for it could be carried out from a safe distance and so keep their identity secret. Noisy though. Attention would be attracted all too quickly by the sound of pistol shots – unless the attack were to be made in some remote place, of course.

Mellors paced the office floor from end to end and back again, his mind racing feverishly over the possibilities. Once he went to the door and turned the handle, meaning to call in Smith and Walker to discuss the matter with him, and then decided against the idea. He was the General. He must present them with a finished plan, coolly and carefully prepared, in an attempt to restore their faith in his leadership. Yes, he must think hard before speaking, but not too long. Time was precious now.

He sat in his stepfather's chair at the desk. John Wood's chair, the chair of a successful cropping master, gave Mellors a feeling of authority, of superiority over other men. From behind a desk such as this he would conduct the manoeuvres of Luddites all over the country, with the courage and panache of a true general. He had a clever, scheming mind, well able to outwit the shrewdest opponent, and by God, Denshaw was to be but the first to fall to his strategy.

Suddenly a thought came into his mind. John Wood had gone into Huddersfield today, Tuesday, because it was a market day, and many manufacturers would be there from whom he might gain business. And Denshaw would undoubtedly be there. It was well known he always went on a Tuesday.

The eager throbbing started in his temples again. To return home to Marsden, Denshaw would have to cross miles of moorland on horseback. Miles of barren heather where few cottages lay and few could witness his passage. Somewhere on the route there must be the perfect spot to intercept him and put an end to his tyranny.

Mellors went over the road in his mind. Denshaw's path would inevitably bring him right past this very place, the cropping shop, when he reached Longroyd Bridge. But that was no good for an attack. The spot was too busy and too many people would be hard by to see. It must be further from the town – up on Crosland Moor, that was the place. And yes, there was a small wood there which would afford an excellent hiding place while

169

they waited for him. And if they used pistols they need not even come out of hiding to make the attack, for there was a low stone wall from behind which they could fire. That was the place. Dungeon Wood was to be Denshaw's deathplace. And today, this evening as he rode home from market.

Mellors grew excited at the thought of such imminent action against the man he despised. Now, who to do the deed? Himself, of course, and just two or three others he could trust implicitly. Too many could wreck the plan. There was Smith and Walker, and they had the advantage of being already here. There was no time to fetch others from further afield if the thing were to be done today.

Thorpe. He wasn't far away – just over the road at Fisher's shop. He could be reached easily. That should be enough. Four of them should be able to deal with Denshaw.

He'd start by talking to Smith. He was the easiest to win over, always victim to Mellors' eloquence, he congratulated himself. Mellors went to the door and called Smith in.

'Sithee, Tom lad, go fetch us a jug of ale, wilt tha, and then bring it in here. I've a matter I want to discuss with thee.'

Smith was not long in returning with the jug of foaming ale. Mellors filled two glasses and handed one to Smith.

'What's this matter tha wants to talk over then, George?' Smith asked eagerly. Mellors walked slowly round the desk and sat in his stepfather's chair. 'Is it another attack?'

'Aye, but of another kind, Tom. We're going to do for old Denshaw.'

Smith's eyes grew wide. Mellors went on before he could protest. 'I've got it all worked out, so there's no fear of us being discovered. We'll shoot him as he nears t' crossroads by Dungeon Wood, from behind t' wall.'

Smith's mouth opened and closed silently, like some stupid fish, thought Mellors, and then he began to splutter. Mellors sighed. He'd known it wasn't going to be easy, but for fifteen minutes he talked coaxingly and persuasively. At length, with the help of the ale, Smith grew less horrified.

'Tha does see as it's absolutely necessary to get shut of t' old bastard, doesn't tha?' Mellors said finally and with a wheedling tone in his voice.

'Aye, I reckon, if tha says so, George.'

'Then tha'll make one o' t' party to do it?'

'Aye, I reckon.'

'Good man.' Mellors rose and came round the desk to clap him on the shoulder. 'I knew I could count on thee, Tom.' Smith glowed uncertainly.

'Now, thee stay here and have another glass and I'll go talk to t' others.'

He smiled on the youth and watched him grow more certain. The lad was evidently proud of being taken into Mellors' confidence first, and of being treated in the master's office at that. Mellors smiled at his own shrewd handling of men, and went out to tackle Walker.

Bill Thorpe was standing outside the door. 'Ah, t' very man I wanted to see!' Mellors greeted him jovially, and watched Thorpe's pleased reaction. There was really nothing to it, persuading others to do his bidding, if one remembered to flatter their vanity. Mellors took him aside out of earshot of the others and put his plan to him. This time he had no need to waste time on subtle persuasion. Thorpe heard him out and then turned a sober face to him. 'I'm with thee, George.'

'Tha art?' Mellors could scarcely hide the surprise in his own voice. It was almost too easy.

'I'm sick to death o' Denshaw and his jeering. Time he were taught that t' Luddites are a force to be reckoned wi'. Tha give me t' pistol, George, and I'm wi' thee.'

Mellors could have hugged him with joy. Instead he left him, to go and tackle Walker, the most likely man to make up the fourth in the party. It was nearing the dinner break before he could find the occasion to talk with him privately, and Mellors was beginning to worry. Walker was a slow-thinking, slow-acting man and was unlikely to be persuaded quickly. And Mellors was determined to strike Denshaw this very afternoon.

Walker was as slow and considering as Mellors had expected. He refused to be forced into a decision instantly.

'After all, t' Avengers didn't get Cartwright,' he mumbled. 'It's not so easy as tha thinks.'

'It's a matter of planning, lad, and I've got it all worked out. We'll not fail,' Mellors assured him confidently. 'Think of John Booth, Ben, and of Hartley, and how their blood was spilt. It's only right we should spill Denshaw's to avenge them.'

'Aye, mebbe so, George, but I mun think about it.'

'There's no time for reflection, Ben. We mun move off this aft if we're to get there i' time.'

'Well, it's not this aft yet. I'll think on it.'

Mellors sighed. 'The bell'll be ringing for drinking time in a minute. Wilt tha think and let me know soon as it's over then?'

Walker looked at the floor. Mellors could

have grabbed his throat in impatient frustration to choke an answer from him. 'Aye,' Ben said at last.

During the break Mellors contrived to have Smith and Thorpe with him by the time Walker came back. If the fellow was still hovering, their added persuasion should do the trick, he reasoned, and to clinch the matter he fetched out the pistols. The sight of them being loaded would help to give the matter an air of decision reached, of finality that could not be gainsaid.

Mellors sat contentedly with his disciples about him, the tins of powder and shot at his side. A shadow fell across him from the doorway. He looked up confidently, expecting to see Walker. It was Will Hall, the young cropper from Liversedge. He leaned against the doorway, smiling. 'I reckon Mester Wood'll be vexed if he finds thee all laking about 'stead o' working,' he commented. 'Isn't he in then?'

'Nay,' replied Mellors. 'Stepfather's out all day. We've serious business to see to, haven't we, lads?'

Walker came in at this point and looked around at the faces nervously. Mellors smiled at him reassuringly.

'Well, Ben lad, hast tha decided? Art tha wi' us?'

Walker nodded. 'If t' others are, I'm wi' thee.'

Mellors slapped his thigh. 'That makes four of us. That's enough for t' job. We'll strike this aft.'

He rammed the powder home in the first pistol and loaded four lead balls. Hall's eyes widened as he watched. 'What the devil art tha doing wi' all that charge, George? Thy pistol'll burst when tha fires that!'

Mellors continued loading the pistols without looking up. 'It needs a powerful charge to make sure of that villain Denshaw,' he said quietly. 'We've agreed to silence him this aft, and tha can join t' party too if tha's a mind to it, Will.'

Hall looked at him aghast. 'Kill Denshaw? Never!' he cried. All the men looked at him. 'No,' cried Hall. 'I'll have nowt to do wi' murder, and that's flat!'

Mellors shrugged his shoulders and went on loading. 'Have it thy way, Will, but we're going on,' he said dryly. 'We've no room in t' party for anyone who hasn't the heart for it any road,' he added, and hoped the sneer in his voice would be noticed by the others. He couldn't afford to let any of them waver now.

He handed a loaded pistol to Walker. 'Here's a pistol for thee, Ben lad. Take it. It's double loaded like mine!' He saw Walker's eyes flicker as he hesitated. Damn the fellow! He was being swayed by Hall's defiance. 'Here, take it!' Mellors snapped. 'It'll not bite thee!' Slowly Walker's hand rose, took the pistol gingerly, and pocketed it.

Hall left abruptly, cursing them for fools. Mellors did not concern himself unduly, for he knew that Hall's loyalty to the Luddite cause would overcome any scruples he might have about murder. If he did not approve, at least he would keep silent.

At last they were ready. 'Get back to thy cropping now, lads,' said Mellors. 'I'll send for thee soon. Keep thy pistols hard by.' He looked them over carefully. 'Three of us i' bottle green close-buttoned suits, and one i' grey. We'll be well hidden amongst t' trees. Good,' he said approvingly. 'Now to your benches, lads, and wait for t' signal.'

The men dispersed. Mellors sat back in his stepfather's chair and poured out more ale. God, but this was going to be a wonderful day for the valley and for the cause! This was going to be a day to remember. He drank deeply, watching the clock with rising impatience.

Soon the dogs of the valley would have Denshaw's guts to tear asunder, and Mellors could not repress his delight.

Thirteen

Jess stood over his loom. His eyes were mesmerised by the flying shuttle, his eyeballs following mechanically the movements to left and right and back again. It was so tiring. He closed his eyes momentarily to rest them, and felt the ache in his limbs and the heaviness and fatigue almost dragging him down to the floor. There could not be many hours of work left.

He turned wearily to look at the clock. Still only mid-afternoon, five hours still to go. He sighed heavily and turned back to his loom. As he did so, a flash of crimson caught his eye. Someone dressed in bright colour had just disappeared into Briggs' office. Whoever it was he would be bound to see as they came out, for a glimpse of any colour was as unexpected as a flash of lightning in the mill. Unrelieved greyness permeated the place, from the metal machinery and dust-shrouded floors to the uncleaned window panes and sombre clothing and peaked, grey faces of the workers. Any brief snatch of colour was a welcome change.

The ache in his stomach was the worst, he decided. There had been so little stew in the pot last night that Jess had feigned lack of appetite so that the girls and Maggie would have a half-filled bowl apiece, and there had been no oatcake left in the creel above the fire this morning before he left. Maggie was still frail; no doubt she'd been too tired and what with the fretful baby she'd had no time or energy to make the oatcake. If only the gnawing pain would stop.

Jess suddenly became aware of the crimson again, growing larger as it approached him. He looked up. Miss Susannah was advancing, a pretty smile on her flushed face.

'Mr Drake!' she called, her voice rising high and clear above the clatter of the machines. Jess straightened and doffed his cap. It was flattering to be addressed as Mister by Mr Denshaw's fine daughter, with her education and breeding and all. 'Mr Drake, could you help me find Mr Briggs. He's not in his office, nor in the loom chamber. Do you know where he is?'

Jess called a child to mind his machine. 'And mind thy fingers,' he warned the little one. ''Appen Mester Briggs is in t' store room, Miss Susannah. Shall I go find him for thee, it being very dirty down there for such fine clothes as thine?'

'If you would please, Mr Drake. Tell him I have a message from Papa. I'll wait in the office.'

Jess walked up the gangway between the machines, nodding a cheerful smile to the little ones who stood, swaying and ashen-faced, over their machines. Poor mites. At least they were spared a strapping while Briggs was out of the way.

He passed Maria's bench and saw she was not there. A sickened feeling passed through his aching stomach, and he hoped she was not with Briggs.

A narrow stone staircase led down to the lower room where the bales of wool were stored. Jess went down and looked about him, but the rows of bales were all that met his eyes. Briggs was not here. He turned to go. Suddenly a sound from the far corner made him stop. It was a girl's giggle.

Jess hesitated. 'Mester Briggs, art tha there?'

There was no answer. 'Mester Briggs, there's a message for thee,' Jess called again. There was a sound of movement, then Briggs' head appeared.

'What is it, Drake?'

'Miss Susannah is here. She has a message for thee from Mester Denshaw seemingly. She's in t' office.'

'Right, I'm coming.' Briggs emerged from the bales and came to join Jess at the foot of the staircase. 'Well, what's tha waiting for? Back to thy machine, lad. Don't take all day!' Briggs snapped, and went ahead of Jess up the steps.

Jess went to follow him, then paused and turned. Was it Maria, still in the corner behind the bales? He hoped it was not, but guessed that it was. Briggs had disappeared from sight. Jess, bedevilled by curiosity, waited.

After a moment there was a rustling, then a girl's dark head appeared. She stood, stretched herself and turned towards him. It was Maria, her bodice fallen about her waist, her firm, full breasts gleaming in the half light, and her hair tumbled and awry. Jess shrank back into the shadow, and as soon as she turned her back and began to pull up her bodice and fasten the buttons, he crept quickly and quietly up the stairs. He did not want her to know he had witnessed her whorelike behaviour, even though he knew she would probably merely shrug and toss her head in defiance. He could not shame her even so.

But still he felt nauseated. He could visualise as clearly as if he had witnessed it, their savage, animal caresses, churning on the stone floor like a couple of pigs in a sty. There was no love between them, he felt sure. Even Maria could not possibly love such a saturnine, brutal sadist as Briggs. And Briggs merely desired the tall, fine-figured girl who gave him the satisfaction his wife could not provide.

The pain in Jess's stomach writhed and stabbed like a knife as he made his way back through the loom chamber to his machine. The child looked up at him. 'Art tha poorly?' he asked Jess listlessly.

Jess shook his head, but as the pain grew wilder and his head began to spin, a flash of crimson appeared at the corner of his eye.

'What is it, Mr Drake? Are you ill?' a sweet, high voice demanded.

Jess could not answer. His legs felt strangely unsteady and he saw the dusty flagstones wheeling and rising and falling.

'Would you like to go home?' the voice asked, but before Jess could refuse, the floor swayed up and hit him. The crimson bent over him.

'Mr Briggs,' a far-away voice said, 'Mr Drake is ill, I fear. See he is sent home and tended,' and then blackness came.

When Jess came to, he found himself slumped in a chair in Briggs' office. Briggs came in.

'Awake at last, art tha? Going to sleep on t' job, indeed! But Miss Susannah insists tha mun go home, so tha'd best go, I suppose. But don't think tha can play that one again, Drake. I'm no fool to be taken in like that. It's thy lucky day, wi' Miss Susannah being so soft and all. Go on, get out and don't clutter t' place up if tha's not doing any work. Get out!'

Jess stumbled to his feet and made for the door. His legs still tried to crumple under him, but he forced himself to go on. As he walked slowly along the length of the loom chamber he saw that Maria was back at her machine, but he averted his gaze so that their eyes did not meet.

Outside, the warm sunlight and fresh breeze restored him quickly and his legs found new strength to walk. He strolled along, uncertain where to go. He did not want to frighten Maggie by appearing so early. Dungeon Wood – he'd go there and sit in the sunlit clearing to rest.

Few people were on the road although it was market day. It was still too early for them to be on their homeward way, but in an hour or so the road would be busy.

He still felt rather queasy, but pushed all thoughts of Maria and her lover out of his mind with resolution. Maria had made it clear that she would lead her own life the way she felt best, so what was the point in his brooding over it? If the thought was distasteful to him, it was best to reject it and pretend it did not exist.

He walked up the hill, past the Warreners, and crossed the road and went up towards the wood. It was cool and dim in the interior, and Jess felt alone and at peace here. The problems of Maria and Mellors and the Ludds seemed far away, remote and unimportant, like the moon and the stars. Here he could relax and forget for a while. He lay down on the grass and dozed.

After a time he awoke. The sun was getting lower and there were voices in the distance. People were coming home from market, no doubt. Perhaps it was time he made a move. He rose and stretched, and as he did so he caught sight of the gnarled old tree. His tree, he had called it as a boy. He remembered how he used to climb up its thick, bark-clad branches to survey the view for miles around, and curl up on a wide fork in its trunk to hide. But that was long ago. He hadn't climbed his tree in many a long year now.

A sudden impulse came over him, unaccountably, to climb his tree just once more, to try and feel again the youthful exuberance and love of life he had felt once. It wouldn't be too hard, even for a man of his age.

He climbed gingerly, and found that indeed the going was easy. He climbed on until he reached the high branch from which he had once surveyed the valley with the pride of a king surveying his dominion, and lay along its broad smoothness, face down. It gave him a glow of deep pleasure to see again the view as he remembered it, the leafy foliage beneath him. Through its interstices he could see to the left the cross roads and to the right, the Warreners and the road ribboning past it and down the valley towards Huddersfield. Far, far away two minute riders on horseback were approaching, not together but some distance apart.

What was that? The sound of voices came to Jess's ears, and they were close by. No one was in sight on the road except for the two distant riders. Then Jess heard footsteps, very near, and a voice saying, 'I've no heart in this matter, let's leave it, at least to another day.'

The voice sounded familiar, but before Jess could place it an angry voice retorted, 'Tha swore to join wi' us and tha will! I'm having no cowards and no backing out, and that's flat!'

Jess's heart missed a beat. It was Mellors' voice, and the first was Ben Walker. What were they doing up here on the moor on a working day?

'Come wi' me, Will,' said Mellors' voice, 'and thee and Tom go just inside t' wood, Ben. Then if we fail, tha can have a go.' Jess could hear but did not see Mellors. He must be still near the low stone wall that skirted the wood. Footsteps crunching beneath him made him hug the branch more closely for fear of being seen.

'This'll do,' said Walker's voice, immediately beneath the tree. 'We can see t' others and t' road from here.'

Four of them – Mellors, Walker, Will Thorpe and Tom Smith. What mischief were they up to now, Jess wondered fearfully. Whatever it was, it must be about to happen soon, for Mellors had just stationed them in their places. Jess craned his neck to peer over the edge of the branch.

Two figures below, one clothed in green and the other in grey, squatted in the shadow of the tree. The one in green was

Walker. Smith leaned over to him.

'I don't like this at all, Ben. Can't tha persuade him to call it off?'

'I've tried, haven't I, and tha saw what he did! He stormed and raved like a madman. I've no mind for it, neither, but he's hell-bent on it and no one'll ever dissuade him now.'

'Dost think we could just sneak away then, and leave him and Will to it? 'Appen he'd not notice.'

'He'd notice, and shoot thee dead if tha tried. Best just sit tight and wait.'

Jess trembled. So Mellors had a pistol with him. What evil plan had he in mind now? Were they lying in wait for some unsuspecting victim? And if so, who?

He looked along the road again. The nearest of the two riders had stopped outside the Warreners and Armitage, the innkeeper, had brought him a glass of ale. The rider tossed it off, fumbled in his pocket and put something into the innkeeper's hand, then waved and rode on up the road towards the wood. His plump figure, sitting deep in the saddle, looked vaguely familiar to Jess, but he was still too far away to recognise. He ambled on, and the further figure approached the inn.

Jess watched the ample figure on horseback shuffling on. The horse was no doubt tired after the long, uphill journey from Huddersfield with such a heavy burden, and the rider seemed to be dozing off in the saddle too for his chin was resting on his chest. As he passed below the wood, towards the crossroads, Jess nearly fell off the branch with shock. A deafening crash rang out that echoed across the valley, and a thin puff of smoke rose over the trees.

A gunshot! Murder! Jess's heart leapt in terror. It was murder Mellors had in his heart! Jess looked anxiously again at the rider. The horse was shying, backing and turning, and its rider was slumped forward on the horse's neck. Of course! It was Denshaw! Mellors had vowed to murder him many times.

Jess was bewildered at his own slowness and confused as to what to do. The harm had already been done. He watched the rider as if hypnotised. A second shot rang out, and as the smoke rose before him again Jess saw through the haze the rider rear up and heard him cry out 'Murder!' It was Denshaw all right, there was no mistaking his voice.

The second rider came galloping up the hill. As he approached Jess heard him call out, 'Haven't you done enough already?'

187

and he galloped on till he reached Denshaw's side.

'Oh God, he's dead, we're done for!' Jess had almost forgotten the two men beneath him. It was Walker's voice, whining in terror. Running footsteps brought Mellors and Thorpe to his side.

'Blast thee, tha didn't fire!' Mellors barked angrily. 'Let's hope Thorpe and me got him.' Jess saw Thorpe then thrust his still-smoking pistol into Ben's hand.

'I don't want it!' Walker cried, and flung the pistol as far as he could. 'I've nowt to do wi' it!'

Mellors grabbed up the pistol. 'Now, now, no panic. We're all in this together. Here, take this two shillings, Ben. Thee and Tom get over to Honley as quick as tha can. Will, thee come wi' me to my cousin Joe's. We'll meet tomorrow. Now run, quick, away from here.'

Jess saw Mellors' and Thorpe's green-clad figures hasten away through the trees. Smith and Walker still stood as if petrified below.

'I'm scared, Ben.' Smith's voice was wavering.

'Aye, they'll never believe that we didn't fire, thee and me. They'll be coming looking for us soon. Let's hide t' pistol's and t' powder horn afore we go, then if we're caught we've no guns to put t' blame on us.'

'Aye.' Smith's voice was eager. Both men knelt and scratched a hole feverishly in a mole-hill, and Jess watched them bury the incriminating evidence hastily.

'Now let's run!

Their running footsteps died away through the wood. Jess turned back to look at the road. The second rider he could see now was Farmer Parr, and he had released Denshaw from the stirrups and was bending over him as he lay on the roadside.

Figures came running from the inn and helped lift Denshaw and carry him back to the inn. As they did so, Jess saw with horror the blood spurting from the lower part of his body and from a large hole in his thigh. Denshaw looked just like Booth on that awful night, his leg almost severed from his body and his life-blood gushing from the enormous wound.

Jess felt too sick with shock and horror to move. He lay there motionless for some time, too numb to know what he should do. He saw the doctor drive up to the Warreners and disappear inside before dusk fell, then Jess moved stiffly, climbing slowly down again to the ground.

No one was about as he trudged up the moor homewards, dizzy with the enormity of what he had seen. Maggie was dozing by the fire and Abigail was rocking baby Seth and crooning to him.

'Tha'rt late, love,' Maggie commented, rising to set a bowl of broth before him. Jess stared at the thin brown liquid, watching the greasy globules on the surface meet and coalesce, and seeing only the grisly sight of Denshaw's wounds. He felt suddenly very sick. Pushing back his chair he rose and tried to hasten to the door, but his legs wavered and turned to water. Sparks exploded in his brain and a red mist swept into the room. Jess called out for help.

'Maggie!' His voice came out thin and reedy as a babe's and his legs twisted and collapsed under him as he fell through oceans of blackness.

Fourteen

The blackness persisted for Jess, broken every now and again by vivid and horrifying nightmares in which he saw Denshaw's bleeding body slump forward in his saddle and heard a terrified voice scream 'Murder!'

The voice howled in agony, screaming for pity and imploring forgiveness, and it finally came to him that the voice was his own.

The blackness was scorching, burning his flesh and drying up his throat till he begged for water, and mercifully a coolness would flow briefly over his scalded throat and moisten his brow. Then instantly the blistering heat would return, burning him up like the flames of hell. It *was* hellfire, tormenting his body for eternity for his silent participation in Denshaw's murder, and again he would hear the pitiful voice crying for forgiveness and release.

Then gradually the searing blackness began to give way to occasional patches of greyness in which faces would bend over him. He clearly saw Maggie's face, drawn and hollow with concern, searching his eyes, and later it was Jenny, her eyes huge with alarm and filled with tears.

In one such moment when the black mist cleared he heard voices raised in argument.

'But Miss Denshaw asked me to call,' a man's voice was saying.

'Very kind of her, I'm sure,' Maggie's stiff voice was replying, 'but we've no brass for doctor's bills.'

'There's no question of payment, Mrs Drake, just let me see him,' the voice went on, quietly enough but firmly.

Maggie appeared at the foot of the bed, her face set hard and her arms folded tightly across her thin chest. 'Here he is.'

A greyhaired gentleman bent over Jess, his eyes clouded and thoughtful. Jess felt his cool fingertips on his forehead and wrist. Then he straightened and turned to Maggie.

'It is indeed the low fever, Mrs Drake, but all being well he should pull through. Take good care not to catch it yourself, however. A good many of my patients have contracted this fever of late, and not all are sufficiently well nourished to withstand it, I fear.'

The voices faded as Maggie and the gentleman went out into the kitchen. Jess was puzzled, but before Maggie could return so he could question her, the blackness had swallowed him up again.

When at last the black heat changed slowly to grey warmth and then gradually to returning clarity, Jess lay awake in his bed and looked about him. It was night, for a lantern burned on the dresser. Maggie was not there.

He became aware that a great weight lay across his feet, and he tried feebly to shake it off and pull his feet free. At length, after much straining and wriggling, the weight began to move. By the lantern light he saw a grey, shrivelled, haggard old woman uncurl slowly and sit up on the end of his bed, rubbing her eyes.

'So tha's come to at last.' To his amazement it was Maggie's voice that issued from the old crone's lips. He screwed up his eyes and peered at her. The grey, lacklustre eyes stared back at him. It *was* Maggie, but she looked a hundred years older than when she had entered with the gentleman. And the strange, hostile look with which she was regarding him was not his Maggie's look. Was his mind still playing tricks with him?

'Dost know me, Jess Drake?' Even her voice was cold and unloving. He opened his cracked lips to reply.

'It's Maggie – isn't it?' He couldn't help the note of doubt.

'Aye, it's me. T' doctor said if tha wakened and knew me, tha'd live. But it's taken thee nigh on three weeks to do it.'

Why was her voice so cold and unconcerned, as if she didn't really care either way? And so old, so aged while he'd been ill? Three weeks, did she say? Three whole weeks he'd lain there in a fever since Denshaw was killed. Jess wondered fearfully whether they'd caught Mellors and the others while he'd lain unconscious. But he couldn't ask Maggie, for that would mean telling her of what he had witnessed. For all she knew, he hadn't yet heard of Denshaw's death.

Oh, it was all too confusing and difficult to think about with his head still feeling so muzzy. He turned his face over into the coolness of the pillow and decided not to think any more yet for a while.

Maggie's voice broke in on his bewilderment. 'Tha's got Miss Denshaw to thank for t' doctor coming to visit thee. She sent him 'cos tha were taken ill at t' mill, seemingly, and she sent thee home. But how she found time to think on a poor loom-minder I'll never know, wi' her own father shot dead i' broad daylight like that.'

Jess's heart thudded. 'Shot?' he repeated.

'Aye, and died t' next day.'

So Denshaw had died from his wounds. It was inevitable, the way he had bled like a pig, blood gushing from his body. Jess shuddered and closed his eyes to try to shut out the mental picture. So Mellors and Thorpe and Smith and Walker were all murderers. And he was an accomplice so long as he remained silent, no better than a murderer himself. Jess groaned.

'Hast tha pain?' Maggie was almost her old self again, showing such concern in

194

her voice.

'Nay, I'm all right, love. Come sit by me and hold my hand a minute.' Jess reached up for her hand but Maggie drew it sharply away.

'Well, if tha's all right, I've work to see to. I can't sit gossiping here all night.' Her voice was so unwarrantedly sharp, Jess looked up at her in surprise.

'What is it, Maggie love? What's amiss?'

'Nowt.' She turned to go, and paused at the doorway, leaning her thin weight wearily against the door jamb. 'They've promised a reward, them magistrates, for anyone as can lead 'em to t' murderers. Two thousand pound, I'm told. Bessie Holroyd had it from one o' t' constables.'

Two thousand pounds! Jess gasped at the almost incomprehensible size of such a sum.

'Aye,' Maggie went on wearily. 'I reckon I could be a rich woman if I told all I knew. But then, I've lived all me life backing thee, Jess Drake, and I'm too old to change me ways now.'

She levered her weight slowly off the doorpost.

'Told? What?' asked Jess, astounded.

She crossed her arms tightly and pressed her lips together. 'I know what I know – and

I'm keeping it to meself so tha's no need to fear. Only never say I wasn't a loyal wife to thee, Jess Drake.'

She left the room abruptly and slammed the door behind her. Jess lay open-mouthed. What did she know? And how? And why did she speak to him so coldly and inimically as if he had committed the murder? If a reward was offered, apparently Mellors and the others were still uncaught and unsuspected. And they would remain so as long as Jess held his tongue.

It was really all too much to comprehend and sort out, and Jess drifted off unhappily into a fitful and dream-filled sleep.

When he awoke his brain felt clearer. Deliberately pushing the shame of his secret knowledge from his mind, he wondered instead what day it was. If not a Sunday, then he ought to be at work at the mill. Too long had he lain idle abed. He wondered how Maggie had managed to cope without his money.

But Denshaw was dead. Was his mill still working after his death? Was there still a job for Jess to return to? And even if young Mr Robert had kept the mill going, was Jess's job still open for him, or had Briggs taken on another man to fill his place by now?

Maggie seemed totally uninterested in his

questions. She sat hunched in her shawl before the low fire. 'I've no notion whether thy place is still awaiting thee or not. Aye, t' mill's still going on. It were shut down for t' day o' t' funeral, that's all.'

Jess decided he'd best go and see for himself. His legs felt groggy under him as he dressed, but he determined not to give in. He must get back to work. Maggie, bless her heart, had made no word of complaint about missing his money. He patted her shoulder tenderly as he passed her chair. Maggie jerked sharply away and glowered at him.

'Tha'd best watch out for thissen if tha's going out,' she said flatly. 'They've been questioning all t' men hereabouts about Denshaw. I sent 'em away from here sharpish, telling 'em tha had the fever and was nigh to death. But they'll get hold of thee when they see thee out.'

'Questioning? Who did they question, Maggie?'

'Every man hereabouts. They all got taken down to Justice Radcliffe's house. Thy fine friend Mellors and all.'

Jess's heart was filled with shame and guilt. Mellors had escaped detection, it seemed. Perhaps the magistrates would never find the culprits – unless someone

197

told tales. Jess shrank from the thought. He was not capable of double-dealing, of betraying an erstwhile friend, but it would be terrible if Denshaw's murderers were never brought to book.

It was a dilemma he preferred not to face. Jess rejected the possibility that the murderers would escape scot-free indefinitely. There was no need for him to tell what he knew. Inevitably they would be caught, sooner or later.

'Art tha going to t' mill then?' Maggie asked quietly.

'Aye. I'll go see Briggs about my job. Where's me muffler, Maggie?'

'Upstairs.' She made no move to fetch it, so Jess climbed the steps with difficulty. In the dim grey light he saw Maria's empty bed. She had evidently left for work already. He looked across at the other pallet. No fair head lay on the pillow. He picked up his muffler and went downstairs.

'Abigail's not there,' he said to Maggie in alarm.

'Aye, that's right.'

'Where is she then?'

'Atkinson's.'

'Where?'

'Atkinson's. I had to put her there to work.'

'But why, Maggie? We agreed...'

'I know what we agreed, but I hadn't thy wage coming in, and how else was I to feed thee t' food t' doctor said, wi' no money?'

'There's Maria – and Jenny.'

'Maria's not much help. And Jenny...' Maggie shrugged uninterestedly and turned her grey face away.

'She were home while I was ill, I remember.'

'Aye, t' first Sunday, not since. Reckon she's been occupied, what wi' t' funeral and all up at t' house. And anyhow she's not paid till t' end o' t' quarter, so I had to put Abbie out.'

'But why Atkinson's, Maggie?' Jess knelt at Maggie's feet and gazed into her haggard face. 'Why Atkinson's, of all places? God knows t' mill is bad enough for children anyhow, but that place is t' worst in t' West Riding by all accounts. I can't bear to think of our Abbie there!'

'There were no room at Denshaw's, and I needed t' brass. That's all there is to it. I'm too tired to argue wi' thee, Jess. She's at Atkinson's, has been for t' past two weeks, and there's an end on it.'

Maggie's voice conveyed the finality she intended it to do, despite the note of utter weariness. Jess got up stiffly from the flagstoned floor and went out without a word. Maybe this evening, if he got his job back, he could reopen the subject and persuade Maggie that Abigail had no need to work any longer. The most urgent task now was to try and secure his job. He set off for Denshaw's mill.

The sun had just risen above the moorland hilltops. It was a bright, clear jewel of a morning, the early sunlight irradiating the tiny crystalline dewdrops ranged along the branches of the trees. The heather crunched underfoot and sprang up confidently, and the air was alive with promise and sparkle. It was the kind of morning that caused one's heart to leap unbidden in hope, no matter what misery and gloom had lately held it prisoner. Jess began to feel calmer as he walked.

Skirting Dungeon Wood, however, guilt and fearful memories returned. Jess averted his eyes from the fateful crossroads where Denshaw had so unsuspectingly encountered his end, and tried to wipe the hideous memory from his mind. But again and again the slumped, bloodstained figure on horseback forced itself back. Jess felt sick every time it returned.

By the time the mill came in sight the fresh spring air had revived him somewhat. He crossed the cobbled yard to the main door. A small child lolled against the wall, chewing the corner of his ragged coat.

'It's locked,' the child said as Jess tried the door. 'Mester Briggs'll not open it yet.' Jess knew Briggs' procedure. Latecomers were locked out for fifteen minutes and then deprived of an hour's wages. He leaned against the wall alongside the child to wait.

The minutes slid slowly by, and then suddenly the door opened. Briggs emerged, smoothing the length of his leather strap.

'Ah, late again art tha, Sykes? I'll teach thee,' he bellowed, and began belabouring the boy. The child screamed piteously as the strap cracked across his bony shoulders, and ran inside. Briggs chuckled and turned to Jess. 'Hello Drake,' he said in surprise. 'Tha's risen from thy sick bed, then? I heard tha were done for.'

Jess smiled feebly. 'I'm as well as ever, Mester Briggs, and good for a hard day's work, if tha's still got me job.' He looked into the other man's steely eyes hopefully. Briggs shook his head.

'Nay, a mill can't wait all these weeks on a loom-minder, Drake. Thy job were gone same day as tha fell ill.'

'Well, is there another job I could do, Mester Briggs? Owt'd suit me, owt at all.'

Briggs leaned on the doorjamb, sunning himself. 'Aye, same as half t' fellows in t' valley, Drake. They'd give their eye teeth for a job, but there's none to be had, and that's a fact.'

'I see.' There was no point in arguing with him. Jess turned to go. Halfway across the yard Briggs hailed him.

'Mind you, if a job should happen to come empty – someone has an accident or summat – maybe I'll bear thee in mind, lad. I'm not promising owt, mind, but fair's fair, and if one o' thine can be reasonable wi' me, it's only right I should do what I can in return.'

He smiled broadly, an ugly, unpleasant smile. Jess realised only too well his implication. 'Thankee, Mester Briggs,' he muttered, and went slowly away.

Somehow the beauty of the spring day had gone sour on him. The guilt on his mind, the thought of Abbie in that terrible mill, and the knowledge that his own future depended on his daughter's whoring, all combined to fill him with misery and repulsion.

Where could he go now? Briggs said there were no jobs to be had anywhere in the valley. Jess was reluctant to return to Maggie having failed in his quest, but neither did he want to go to the wood and think. The thought of Dungeon Wood now was unbearable, saturated as it was with the memory of Denshaw's blood.

The inn, perhaps, for a drink? But in the inn there would be soldiers and prying people who might ask questions. He remembered then Maggie's warning that he might be taken for interrogation, and decided it would be safer to return home after all.

Past the wood, half-way up the road to his cottage, a hurrying figure in a shawl came running down towards him. He recognised Mrs Benson, a near neighbour.

'Mester Drake!' she called as she came up to him, breathless and pink-paced. 'Tha'd best get home, quick. Thy Maggie's not well.'

Jess's heart skipped a beat. If Maggie had sent someone for him, then she was truly ill. Maggie was not one to complain unless it were bad.

'Did Maggie send thee for me?'

'Aye, she said to come and mind t' babe.'

'What ails her, Mrs Benson?' The thought crossed his mind that Mrs Benson could have cared for the child and hardly noticed, having several of her own already.

'I'm not sure, Mester Drake, but if it's what I think, I'm afraid I'll be keeping clear o' thy house. Not that I don't think a lot o' thee and Maggie, but I've children of me own to care for, tha knows.'

'I know, but what dosta think it is, Mrs Benson?'

'It's fever, I'll be bound, low fever, Mester Drake, and there's not many of us so lucky as thee to escape that.'

Fifteen

Life was beginning to revert to its usual smoothness at Brackenhurst after the unexpected and untimely death of its owner. Robert was beginning to feel irritated once more by the prickling monotony of it all. For a time it had almost been fun. Of course he had been as shocked and horrified as Susannah over Father's terrible death, but it had brought the consolation of making them the centre of attention and pity for a time.

Well-to-do families round about who had hitherto not recognised the Denshaws among their close circle, no doubt having heard of Robert's rakish adventures in London, he preened himself to think, had suddenly become very solicitous and charming. Ingratiating mothers had called to present their cards and sympathy, as well as their fat, nubile daughters, and Robert had begun to hope for a little sport. But Susannah had politely but firmly declined their company and services, and the promise held out to him had dissipated into the spring mists.

Weeks had passed since the funeral, and the glowing interest in them as a family had died away. Callers at Brackenhurst were less frequent, except for Captain Northcliffe, of course, and he practically lived in the house. In fact it was Sukey's almost total preoccupation with him that made life so blank for Robert. It was all very well for her, but what had he to occupy him?

He had paid a couple of visits to the dirty mill as duty had demanded of him, but it was evident that no more could be expected of him. Briggs was obviously capable of running the place better than he, and as long as he and his assistants kept the workers hard at it with their whips, and Susannah saw to the marketing side of the business, Robert, so far as he could see, was quite expendable.

All he wanted of the mill was the money it produced. The solicitor had said that his father's will was quite straightforward and uncomplicated so the matter should be completed without delay. At last Robert would have money in his pockets. London was in sight at last. He must broach the subject of his leaving to Sukey as soon as possible. That was only a matter of form, of course, for she could not prevent his departure as Father had done for so long.

He timed the moment to introduce the subject to coincide with the satisfied smile Sukey always wore after Northcliffe's departure in the evening. The smile faded quickly.

'So soon after Papa's death, Robert? What will people think? It's most inconsiderate of you to think of leaving yet, when there are still so many problems to iron out. I think you should wait a little longer.'

'It matters little what you think, Sukey.' Robert smiled lazily. After all, he was master now, and there was no one who could deny him. Susannah rounded on him.

'Don't you want to wait to see Papa's murderers caught and punished? Don't you want to see justice done? How can you think of going off to enjoy yourself while he lies hardly cold in the ground, and as yet un-avenged!'

Susannah's eyes blazed at him. Robert felt piqued but determined to remain cool. He shrugged indolently.

'It is possible they'll never be discovered,

and what then? Do you want me to remain here all my days? And whether they're caught or not, the fact still remains that Father is dead. I can't bring him back, you know.' Nor would he want to, Robert added inwardly. Life held far more opportunities now.

'I know.' Susannah flung herself petulantly into a chair, tears filling her eyes. Oh Lord, he hoped she wasn't going to start that woman's stuff, blubbing all over the place. She could keep that for Northcliffe; no doubt he would rise gallantly to the occasion.

'Anyway,' Robert went on casually, 'the way things are going, it seems to me you and young Northcliffe will make a match of it soon. You can have the house to yourselves. He knows all about the wool business too, so he'd be a better adviser for you than I can be.'

'That's all you care about!' Her voice registered scorn as well as anger. 'Captain Northcliffe and I can tend your business, just so long as the money flows in for you to spend! Well let me make it clear, I do not propose to marry Charles just in order to protect your business interests, so there!'

'He has asked you then?'

She looked at the floor. 'No, not yet.

207

Though I think he has it in mind. But I warn you now, I shall refuse him if you desert me. What right have you to leave two defenceless women alone in a big house like this? Since Jenny left, there's only Hannah and me if you go.'

'Jenny? Left?' Robert tried to keep the guilty tremor out of his voice. He had almost forgotten that shameful night in the shock of the murder and funeral and all.

'Yes, didn't you know?' Susannah's voice was sulky now. 'About a week after Papa's funeral. She just suddenly – wasn't there one day. Hannah doesn't know where she went or why.'

'Back home, probably,' said Robert. 'The shock of Father's horrible death, I should think.'

'A week after the funeral? The shock took a long time to register in that event. Hannah said she'd been acting strangely, all silent and secretive, but she'd no idea what was wrong.'

'Sickening for the fever, perhaps. There's been a lot of it about, I hear.' Robert shuddered at the thought of touching a vile, dirty creature already perhaps smitten with the contagion. He rubbed his hands involuntarily on his breeches.

'Possibly,' Susannah sighed. 'Anyway,

she's gone. I've had so much to do I haven't had time to send to enquire after her.'

'Then I shouldn't bother, my dear. You can no doubt find another and better maid elsewhere.'

'But you won't leave me and Hannah alone, will you, Robert? It's not safe.'

'Safe? Nonsense!' Robert retorted. 'If it's the Ludds you fear, Sukey, their day is done. I know they had the people's sympathy while they confined their activities to machine-breaking, but murdering Father has alienated everyone's sympathies completely. There's not a man in the valley now who would shield a Luddite. Their group is smashed, finished, I'm sure of it. They'll never lift a finger again.'

Susannah sighed. 'I know. You're quite right, Robert, but I don't like to see you go so soon. Wait just a little while, won't you, until matters are more – settled?'

'Until you and Northcliffe are married?' Susannah blushed becomingly. Robert felt he could afford to be magnanimous, now he had won the argument. 'Very well, only make it soon.'

'He hasn't proposed to me yet,' Susannah protested.

'But he will, you'll see to that, I know.' Robert, like his father, knew his sister's managing ways usually succeeded. Only in the matter of his going to London had she, for once, failed.

Jess bent solicitously over Maggie's crumpled figure, huddled deep in her shawl by the fire.

'How art tha feeling now, love?' he asked her tenderly.

Maggie shuddered. 'I'm cold, Jess, so cold,' she moaned.

He laid a hand on her brow, smoothing back the wisps of grey hair. Her forehead was hot and dry to his touch. Mrs Benson was right, it was a fever right enough, but possibly not the low fever which robbed so many folk of at least one member of the family.

'Tha'd best get to bed then,' he urged her softly. 'Come lass, and I'll heat thee a brick to warm thee.' Maggie rose wearily and went without argument into the bedroom. She was certainly sick, not to refuse to go to bed.

'Tha'll have to see to Seth,' she mumbled, pointing a feeble arm in the direction of the basket on the floor. The child lay quiet, so Jess decided to see to Maggie first.

'Later,' he promised. 'Now get into bed.'

It took Jess some time to prepare the broth

for her, for he was unaccustomed to cooking, and the few withered vegetables he could find would barely make a nourishing meal. At length, however, he took her a dish into the bedroom. Maggie lay fully dressed under the blanket, shivering so violently that the bed frame shook.

'Here, love, have some of this good broth I've made thee,' Jess murmured, sliding an arm under her shoulder. Maggie turned her head to the wall.

'I've no appetite for food. Save it for t' lasses.' Her voice was barely a whispered croak, and Jess could feel her wasted body shaking in his arms. He laid aside the bowl and gave her a sip of water from a cracked cup instead. After, Maggie licked her lips with a swollen, blackened tongue and lolled back. Her eyes were glazed and expressionless, and Jess felt fear rising inside him.

A sudden rap at the cottage door took him by surprise. He rose quickly, eager to welcome whoever it might be, who might possibly be able to help. It was the doctor.

'Hullo?' said the doctor in surprise, his whip handle raised ready to knock again. 'Up and about again, eh, Drake? I'm glad to see you made so speedy a recovery after all. That's one less call I shall have to make from now on. Wish all my patients had your resilience, Drake.'

He smiled cheerily and turned to go. 'Nay, nay, wait on a moment, doctor,' Jess blurted suddenly, fearful lest the doctor should leave if he did not speak soon enough. 'My Maggie – she's ill – I fear she has the fever now. Wilt tha look to her, doctor? I've no money,' Jess looked at the floor uncomfortably, but decided this was no time for pride. 'I've none just now, that is, but I'll find work again soon, I know I shall. If tha'll do summat for Maggie, doctor, I'll see tha's paid, I swear I will.'

The doctor made no reply but simply brushed Jess aside and strode into the little cottage, stooping to duck under a low lintel. He made straight for the little bedroom, and leaned his height low over the bed. Jess watched from the door. Maggie neither spoke nor stirred.

Eventually the doctor straightened and came thoughtfully out, drawing Jess with him.

'You're right, Drake, she has the low fever. But she's very weak after nursing you and the baby so long. I know she hardly slept all the time you were ill, and all the food she had she gave to you. The result is, she's no strength left to fight the fever. I'm afraid the outlook is very serious, Drake. You must prepare yourself.'

'But is there no physic tha can give her, doctor? Owt that can cure her, no matter what the cost?' Jess's voice was high with fear.

The doctor shook his head sadly. 'I'm afraid there is no miracle cure, not even for the King himself. Good food, careful nursing could do the trick, but she's so weak, so frail...'

Jess put his hands over his face. He could not bear the doctor to see the tears that sprang to his eyes. Dear Maggie, sacrificing all her strength to save him, and there was nothing he could do in return to save her! The doctor put his hand gently on Jess's shoulder.

'Don't give up, man. It's possible – just possible, mark you – that she could pull through yet. If the will to live is strong enough, she could fight it off and confound us all. I've seen it happen, but don't bank on it, Drake. Pray and hope.'

'About thy bill...' Jess began, stumbling after him.

He gave Jess's shoulder a final, reassuring pat and strode out of the door.

'No bill,' said the doctor curtly, mounting his horse and turning it about. 'There is no treatment I can give your wife, Drake, so

213

there will be no bill. Good day to you.' He cantered off down the lane.

Maggie was still lying staring vacantly at the raftered ceiling and shivering when Maria came home from the mill.

'What ails her?' Maria asked, casting a peremptory glance at the bed.

'The fever. Doctor says she's bad.'

'Oh. They all are wi' that.' She was looking around the room. Jess noticed she had not yet taken off her shawl.

'There's broth for thee over t' fire,' he told her, but Maria was not listening. 'Leave some for Abigail.'

'Abigail? Oh, she can have it all. Listen father, I've only come home to pack me things. I'm leaving.'

Jess looked up. 'Leaving? What dosta mean?'

Maria sighed with a feigned attempt at patience. 'Now don't start arguing wi' me, father, I'm leaving and that's that. I'm going to Mester Briggs if tha really wants to know, cos he's asked me to.'

She turned and began picking up her clothes, as though to signify that the news had been broken and that was the end of the matter. She did not want to hear her outraged parents' protests or refusal.

But Jess did not feel outraged, only disappointed and panic-stricken. One should be able to expect some measure of loyalty and backing from one's own child.

'But thy mother's ill, sorely ill, Maria. Tha can't leave at a time like this!' He could hear that his voice sounded like a petulant child. Maria turned on him quickly.

'I can leave when I like – and I'm choosing now because I've just been asked! I may not get the chance again if I refuse, and who in their right mind would choose to live here, like this, when I could be at Briggs' and eat regular and have clothes on me back?'

She paused and glanced at her silent mother. 'I'm sorry me mam's ill, of course, but she'll get over it same as thee.' Her voice was less harsh and more reasonable now. Jess tried again.

'What of Mrs Briggs then?'

'What of her? She's very ill, dying they say. Briggs needs me to mind her and all his childer.'

'And if Mrs Briggs does die?'

'Then he'll need me all t' more, won't he?'

'And will he marry thee then?'

Maria shrugged. 'Who knows? He's never said. But whether he does or not, I'll eat and be warm as long as I'm there.'

She finished putting her belongings together into a large kerchief and tied the knot

215

securely. Maggie turned over and looked at the girl listlessly.

'Art awake, love?' Jess said softly, coming to her side. 'Maria's leaving, Maggie, going to live at Briggs'. But don't fret thissen, Abigail and I'll see to thee.'

Maggie looked at her eldest daughter vacantly, shrugged her skinny shoulders and turned away.

'Tha see, me mam doesn't mind,' said Maria defiantly. 'So there's nowt to fret over, is there?'

Jess sat listlessly in the chair. 'We'll miss the money sorely, Maria. There's nobbut thee and Abigail bringing t' brass home now.' It hurt him to speak of little Abbie in the mill.

'Tha's well enough to get back to t' mill thissen now. I stayed all t' time tha were ill, tha knows.'

Jess looked at her wonderingly. She obviously did not know. 'Briggs won't have me back,' he said quietly.

Maria's jaw dropped. 'He won't? He didn't tell me that.' She prodded the door-jamb with her toe for a few moments and then turned to Jess. 'I'll speak to him about that, Father. He's a fair enough man when he's not full of ale, and I reckon he'll do me a favour if I ask him. Never fear, I'll do what

216

I can for thee.'

A fleeting smile crossed her face and she turned to go. Jess felt sorry for his ill-feelings towards her and called out after her. 'God bless thee, lass, and I hope tha prospers.'

He heard the cottage door slam behind her, shivering the glass in the window frames. Minutes later he heard the door open again, and hastened to it eagerly. Had Maria changed her mind and come back after all?

But it was Abigail who stood just inside the door, her usually erect figure bent and cowed. She held her shawl with tight, nervous fingers to her throat, and her eyes were wide and fear-filled. A long bruise reddened across her cheek, and she wore the stupid, vacant look of an imbecile.

Jess cried out aloud. This was what the mill had done to his precious lively, laughing angel! He sobbed gently as he hugged her tense little body to him.

Sixteen

When Jess went to bed that night his heart lay heavy within him. The foul, nauseating memory of Denshaw's murder which he had tried to push to the back of his memory had been deadweight enough on his mind, over-burdened as it was with the guilty knowledge of his inaction. But now with the added worry of Maggie's danger and Maria's indifference and selfishness, and Jenny's too it would seem, life was grimmer than ever. And the final blow, seeing the change the mill had wrought in his bright, beautiful Abigail, made his heart bleed as it had never done before.

She had not complained, the brave little thing, as she sat and supped her broth, only twitched her mouth every now and again involuntarily as the effort of eating gave pain to her bruised face.

'Who hit thee, lass?'

'T' overseer.'

'Why?'

'I were weary. I nearly fell asleep.'

That was all she had said, no grumbling, no complaining. How like her mother she was, proud enough to bear all without whining. And the worst of Jess's bitterness lay in knowing that there was nothing, nothing at all he could do to alleviate her suffering, to save her from the mill. Her money was vital. She would have to go on, day in, day out, till she wed or died, grey and prematurely aged like Maggie.

He lit a candle and saw Abigail into bed. The child's eyes were closed before her head touched the pillow. Jess went back downstairs and into the bedroom, where Maggie was lying wide awake. She watched him as he entered with the candle.

'How dosta feel, lass? Better?'

'Middling. But I'm still cold.'

Jess drew out his pallet, meaning to sleep on the floor as she had done while he was ill. Her voice came, cracked and pathetic, from the bed. 'I'm bitterly cold, Jess. Come warm me up.'

That was the first time since Seth was born that Maggie had invited him to lie by her. Wordlessly Jess undressed, blew out the candle, and crawled into bed. Maggie huddled close to him and Jess put his arm protectively around her. She was still very hot.

He lay still and silent for a while, unwilling to disturb Maggie if she wanted to sleep. But he could hear by her breathing that she lay awake too. After some time he spoke.

'Maggie, love, can I talk to thee? Like in the old days? I've that much on me mind.'

'Aye, if tha wants.'

A warm glow started to spread through Jess at once. The problems would not be solved easily, if at all, but at last, after a long silence between them, Maggie and he were going to be able to talk, closely and intimately, as a man and wife were meant to do. And that meant a great deal to Jess. No longer would he feel so alone and defenceless with Maggie to share his tribulations.

He started to talk about Abigail, the bruise on her pretty face and the cruelty of men who could treat young children so. He talked of the gaiety that had gone from her and was quick to add that of course Maggie could have done little else in the circumstances than send her into the mill.

All this time Maggie said not a word. He went on to talk of his disappointment in Maria, deserting her mother at a time like this. And his surprise that Jenny had not been home to see how they fared. Surely she had not become so selfishly immersed in her newfound good fortune that she had forgotten her loyalty to them already. Still Maggie did not comment.

Of the other vast, insuperable problem on his mind, the witnessing of Denshaw's murder and his subsequent silence, Jess could not bring himself to speak at all. He was saved from it, however, by a faint, squeaking sound like a kitten's mew, here in the bedroom. He sat up.

'What were that?'

Maggie did not answer. Jess went to swing his legs out of bed. 'I'd swear I heard a kitten here. Didst hear it too, Maggie?'

'Aye. It were t' babby.' Her tone showed no interest at all. Jess was confounded.

'Seth? Were it him? What's wrong wi' him?'

'Same as all of us, he's hungry.' Her voice was still completely flat and emotionless.

'Can't tha give him owt then?'

'I've nowt for him, neither milk nor food. And what's t' use any road? He's bound for t' graveyard soon.'

Jess was horrified and felt almost physically sick at her apparent unconcern. How could a mother speak so of her own child? 'Maggie, don't talk that way, it's sinful,' he cried.

Maggie shrugged. Jess could not understand what was happening. The mewing had ceased and he paused, uncertain whether to get up and see what he could do for the child, or lie down again and try to talk sense to Maggie. As he lay slowly down and pulled the blankets over him, a sudden, cracking sound at the window made him start upright again.

'What's that?' Maggie did not move. The rattling sound came again. 'It's someone throwing stones at t' window! Who could that be?'

He rose quickly and pulled on his breeches, then threw on his jacket and went to open the outer door.

'Who's there?' he called out as he unlatched.

A gruff voice on the other side replied, but he could not hear the words or identify the owner. The bolt drawn, Jess threw back the door. A shadowy figure some paces away came forward.

'Come outside, Jess. I want a few words wi' thee in private.'

There was no mistaking George Mellors' voice. From force of habit Jess obeyed the tone of command, and he pulled the door closed behind him.

'What dosta want wi' me?' he asked, filled with curiosity and a tinge of fear. Mellors had kept his distance since Jess's abnegation of the movement on the day of Booth's funeral, and to the best of Jess's knowledge, he had no suspicion of what Jess knew about Denshaw's murder. What could have brought him up here in the middle of the night?

'I hear as tha's been ill, Jess lad.'

'Aye, I were, but I'm well now.' Jess was still wondering. Mellors would never come on a midnight visit simply to enquire after a friend's health.

'Fever, they said. Delirious, they said.'

'Aye, mebbe. I've no recollection.' Whatever it was he came about, Jess wished he would get on with it. It was damnably cold out here, only half-dressed, even for May.

'I've heard tha were babbling i' thy fever about a murder tha'd seen, about pistols and blood and all.'

Jess's heart thudded. So Mellors did know that Jess had witnessed it. He decided to fence a little.

'Who told thee that? Who heard me say it?'

'Never mind how I know, let it suffice that I know.'

'People say owt when they're delirious. What dosta know?'

Mellors hesitated. 'It seems tha knows more than is good for thee about a certain murder that took place hereabouts lately.'

'Denshaw, tha means?'

'Aye. And how tha came to be a witness I'll never know, but one thing's for certain. Tha mun never speak of it to anyone.'

'I've not been asked.'

'Aye, that's the danger. Every man in t' valley has been questioned by t' magistrates, barring thee, 'cos tha were sick i' bed. But I reckon as Radcliffe will remember thee and call thee in yet, so I've come to warn thee.'

'Warn me?'

'Well, let me say remind thee then. Remember tha swore a sacred oath never to tell owt tha knew.'

'Aye, I know.'

'And art willing to keep thy word?'

Jess hesitated. He knew if he were questioned it would be only right and honest to give his evidence, to see the wrongdoers brought to trial. It was a man's duty to uphold right and justice. But on the other hand, he had given his word to this man, an oath taken publicly and in good faith. He could not respect himself again if he dishonoured his vow.

'Well?' There was anxious impatience in Mellors' voice, rasping and irritable.

'Aye, I'll keep silent.'

'Good man. I knew we could rely on thee, even if tha has deserted us. I know tha weren't a traitor.'

His hand fell on Jess's shoulder in the old, familiar manner. Jess shrugged it off instantly in distaste. He wanted no warm, friendly commerce with a murderer.

'If that's all tha wants I'll go back to me wife now,' he said, making for the door.

Mellors accompanied him to the doorway. 'Only remember, lad, when tha's face to face wi' Radcliffe and tha might come to think differently, the ending o' that oath we took.'

'Ending? What art tha talking about?'

'That bit about traitors. One word that could give us away could lead to thy own death, Jess Drake, for t' others would hunt thee down and murder thee as surely as tha would be giving us to t' hangman's noose. It'd pay thee to remember that if ever tha feels tempted to open thy mouth.'

'I've promised thee, haven't I? Isn't that enough?' Jess cried, desperately anxious to be rid of this man.

'Aye, of course. Well, good night to thee, and I hope tha's heard t' last o' t' matter, Drake.'

He strode quickly away into the darkness. Jess stood in the doorway a moment, his heart pounding with anger and humiliation. A promise had been extracted from him. Ever since the murder his mind had refused

225

to consider what he should do, reluctant to be obliged to make a decision, and now, in a few moments, the decision had been forced upon him.

It would not matter if the decision was the right one, but his conscience was heavy and sore. He was angry with himself for being weak enough to agree to make a promise he knew to be wrong.

Blast them all! The world was determined to force problems upon him that he was unable to cope with. As if he hadn't enough to worry about already!

He pushed the whole matter deliberately from his mind. He would think about it later, when Maggie was well again. Not tonight. Tonight he must tend Maggie carefully.

Jess climbed wearily back into bed. Maggie, to his surprise, did not ask who had thrown stones at the window, or what the caller wanted. That at least was a relief. But then, maybe it would be best if he were to tell her all, of what he had seen that fateful day in Dungeon Wood and of Mellors' threat if Jess spoke of it.

'Maggie,' he said tentatively. 'There's summat I want to tell thee, if tha's not too tired.'

'Go on.'

'It's about Denshaw and how he were

murdered.'

Maggie sighed. 'I wondered if tha were ever going to tell me.'

'Tell thee? What?'

'What tha'd done. I knew all t' time.'

'How could tha know? Did I talk of it while I were ill?'

'Many a time. Tha frightened me wi' all thy talk o' blood and pistols and all. Now go on, tell me.'

'Well, that's all. I saw him shot dead.'

'Saw him? Pulled t' trigger, more like.'

'Nay, Maggie, not I!' Jess started upright. 'Tha doesn't think I did it, dosta?'

'Then who did?'

'Mellors – and Thorpe, I think. Smith and Walker were below t' tree I were hid in, and they never fired a shot. It were t' others.'

Maggie lay silent. Jess gripped her shoulder. 'Tha does believe me, doesn't tha?'

She sighed. 'I believed tha had t' courage to speak t' truth to me, thy wife, if to no one else.'

'But I didn't shoot him, Maggie, I swear! Tha must believe me, I didn't do it!' Jess's voice rose shrill among the rafters. For Maggie, always trusting and loyal, to lose faith in him now was too much!

Maggie turned away from him and faced the wall.

'Maggie, say tha believes me!'

Her voice came back, low and toneless. 'I no longer know who to believe, nor do I care. I never thowt Maria'd leave us neither. I never thowt I'd bear childer to watch 'em die. There's nowt left to believe in, nor work for. I'm tired o' trying, Jess, and that's the truth. There's nowt.'

'There's me, love. I need thee.'

'Aye, so I thowt. But I heard thee prating of death and murder. Tha's not the man I knew. I can't believe in thee now. There's nowt left.'

'Maggie, I swear to thee on t' Bible, I had nowt to do wi' Denshaw's death! I only saw it happen!'

Maggie rolled over and regarded him solemnly. 'I'm not daft, Jess Drake. There's a reward out for two thousand pound for any man as'll tell who t' murderer's are. That much money'd see us all rich to t' end of our days and we'd never want for another mouthful again. Yet thy babby's dying of hunger, thy little lass is belted black and blue, and all t' time tha's kept silent. And why else if tha's not one o' t' murderers thissen?'

She rolled away again. Jess sat, stunned and horrified. He must clear himself, if only to Maggie! 'I took an oath of secrecy, love,' he protested.

'I don't want to talk of it any more. I'm that tired, and so cold.' Her voice was low and pitiful. Jess took her in his arms, but she lay stiff and shivering.

Far into the night Jess spoke to her, softly and persuasively, telling her of his innocence and of his undying love for her and their children. After a time Maggie's shivering stopped, but she spoke no words in acknowledgement of what he said. He talked on, persuading her that her faith in him was not unfounded, begging her to believe in him again and so restore his confidence. So long as she loved and trusted him, he would do aught she wished, even break his vow and speak if she wanted it, though it would grieve his conscience.

Still no answer came. Jess hugged her stiff body closer, willing her to relax and relent. He wanted above all to restore her faith in him, in life, and in hope for better things.

Finally, worn out by work and worry and long hours of talking, Jess fell asleep. But his sleep was troubled by tormenting dreams and it was broad daylight when he awoke with a start. Seth was making the mewing noise again.

Jess withdrew his cramped arm from under Maggie's weight and sat up. 'I'll have to go to work, I'm late,' he said to her. 'Art awake, lass?'

She did not answer. Jess took hold of her shoulder.

'I'll go see if Abigail's up,' he said. 'Art listening, Maggie?'

Still no answer. Jess pulled her arm. Maggie's head rolled over and she stared unseeingly at the ceiling. Jess bit back a cry of horror. Her eyes were glazed and clouded.

'Maggie! Maggie!'

She was not breathing. She was dead in his arms. Jess refused to believe it. She could not die like that, angry and hurt with him, and still believing him to be a murderer!

The doctor's words rang in his ears. 'If the will to live is strong enough, she could fight it off.' If the will to live were strong enough. And Maggie had said she'd lost the will to live after all she'd gone through.

But the bitterest thought was that he himself had delivered the final blow to her fragile frame. Believing him a murderer had killed her lifelong trust in him, and he had not been able to persuade her of his innocence. He himself had killed his workworn, devoted wife. Oh Maggie!

He flung himself across her thin, unyielding body and abandoned himself to sobbing, engulfed in grief and guilt.

Seventeen

Jess remained for a long time over Maggie's body, pouring out his life's anguish and remorse, and he lost track of time altogether. It was the gentle sound of the baby's mewling cry that brought him back to his senses. He rose stiffly, wiped the tears from his face with the back of his sleeve, and bent to look at the little one in his basket.

The child's fist was pushed into the tiny mouth, which puckered and pulsated as the little jaws tried to suck sustenance from its fingers. Finding nothing, the mouth opened and wailed piteously again.

Jess felt helpless. Feeding a bairn was woman's work. He glanced at the wasted body in the bed in mute appeal, but Maggie would never be able to help again. Maria too would be too fully occupied with Briggs' seven children and sick wife to come to his aid. Jenny! She perhaps would come if Miss Susannah would permit it.

With a plan of action thus in mind, Jess bestirred himself to tidy his hair and clothes

231

and wash his face. He tried hard not to look at the bed, for the sight of Maggie's cold body, stiff in relentless disbelief of him, wounded him deeply.

He wondered whether to leave baby Seth here in his basket or carry the child up to Brackenhurst with him, for there was no one else to mind him. Unless Abigail was still here. He had not heard her leave for the mill.

Jess went through into the living-room and met Abigail just descending the stairs and rubbing her eyes.

'What o'clock is it, Father? I fear I've overslept and I'm late for me work.' Her face looked crumpled and harrassed and the bruise showed blue against the pale skin. Jess put his arm around her scrawny shoulder.

'Never mind, lass, I've need of thee at home today.'

She looked up at him, but her look held none of the expectant animation it would once have done. It was a worn, disinterested look.

Jess sat on a chair and drew the child to him. 'Listen, lovey, I've bad news for thee. I fear thy mother has died, lass. Nay, don't take on so, don't cry. Tears'll not bring her back. Thy baby brother needs thee to mind him while I go fetch Jenny home. Wilt be a good lass and care for him while I'm gone?'

Abigail nodded dumbly and flung her arms about his neck. For a moment Jess yielded to her loving warmth, and then he rose quickly.

'I'll not be long, love.'

It was only as Brackenhurst came into sight and Jess turned up into the long drive that he realised he was approaching the house of the man he had watched so cold-bloodedly struck down. The feelings of guilt pushed back into the remotest corners of his mind slithered quickly to the forefront.

He was about to confront the servants, possibly even the family of the man he had failed to see avenged. He was about to ask them to return him his daughter in his need, but he could never return to them the father they had doubtless loved, whatever his apparent failings and misdeeds in the eyes of the valley folk.

Jess's steps faltered, but he quickened his pace again. Seth needed Jenny, and he must put the baby's needs before his own discomfiture. Jess could not make himself approach the main door of the house, but sidled instead to the back door.

He could hear a woman's voice singing as she worked in the kitchen. He knocked timidly, and presently the door was opened by a plump, florid-faced woman.

'Whatever tha's peddling, we want none,' she said briskly, wiping the flour from her hands with a cloth.

'I'm none peddling, I've come to see my lass, Jenny.'

The woman stopped as she was about to close the door in his face. 'Jenny, tha says? She's not here.'

'But she must be.'

'She's not, I tell thee. Didst say tha were her father?'

'Aye.'

'Well then, thee tell us where she is. She upped and off wi'out a word to anyone, the ungrateful lass, after all Miss Susannah's done for her.'

Jess's heart banged uncertainly against his ribs. He wasn't hearing aright. Jenny had not been home for some weeks now – she must be here! He started to tell the woman so, but she cut him short.

'I tell thee she's gone, and that's all I know!'

'What is it, Hannah?' a gentler voice interrupted. Jess recognised it instantly. It was the kindly voice of Miss Susannah. She appeared behind Hannah, looking as delicate as china with her pretty pink face and floating chiffon dress. 'Why, it's Mr Drake,' she exclaimed. 'I'm glad to see you are fully recovered and about again. Pray tell me, has Jenny been taken sick of the fever too? I have missed her sorely since she left.'

So the woman had been telling the truth – Jenny was gone. But where? Jess's mind went over the possible answers confusedly, but could not think of any place.

'Beg your pardon, Miss? Oh, no, Jenny hasn't got the fever. Leastways, not so far as I know. When dost tha say she left?'

'Oh, it must be two weeks or more, isn't it Hannah? Yes, it was very soon after my father's funeral.' Her voice dropped a semi-tone as she mentioned her father, and Jess felt himself redden.

'Well, I thank thee for what tha's done, Miss Susannah – for me as well as for Jenny. I'll not trouble thee any longer.'

He turned to go. 'But where will you look for her, Mr Drake, if she doesn't come home?' Susannah called after him.

'I don't know. I'll think of somewhere,' he muttered. 'Thankee, and good day to thee.'

He blundered aimlessly down the drive and out along the road. From force of habit his footsteps guided him towards home, but half way along the road he stopped. It was no use expecting Abigail to cope with the

235

baby – she was as ignorant as he about how to deal with a tiny child. He would have to go and ask Maria.

By the time he reached the little row of cottages where Briggs lived it was almost mid-day. Presumably Maria would be at the house and not at the mill if she was caring for Briggs' children and his sick wife. A savoury smell drifted through the air as he knocked at the door.

Squeals of laughter and howls of dismay came from within. Jess heard the sound of a woman's voice and smacking before the door finally opened and Maria's tousled head appeared. She looked hot and flustered and angry.

'What dosta want here, father?' she demanded in surprise. 'I'd a thowt tha'd be at work or nursing me mam. What dosta want of me?'

'Maria, thy mam died this morning.'

'Oh.' She looked startled and her face softened just for a moment, then hardened quickly again. 'Well?'

'Canst tha come home, love?'

'Home? Why?'

'Seth needs someone to look after him.'

A child tugged at Maria's skirts and howled some piteous complaint about his elder brother boxing his ears. Maria turned and boxed the ears of the laughing, mischievous child behind her, and he stopped pulling tongues and began to wail.

Maria uttered a huge, impatient sigh. 'Tha can see I can't come, father. They're all waiting to be fed, and Briggs himself'll be here in a minute. He'll be mad at the state the house is in. Wi' this wild lot I can't get nowt done, what wi' her calling for attention every five minutes too.'

Maria glanced over her shoulder nervously. 'I'm sorry father, but I chose to come here, for reasons I told thee. I'll not change me mind now. I'm sorry about me mam, but as to Seth – well, there's Jenny. Go see Jenny. I'll have to go now.'

'Jenny's gone!' Jess cried before she could close the door on him.

Maria turned. 'Gone? Where?'

'I don't know. They tell me at Brackenhurst she just disappeared.'

Maria clicked her tongue. 'She did right. T' way things are going, I think I'll up and off into nowhere soon too. I'm sorry, but there it is. I'm not coming, I can't.'

A door at the back of the house slammed and Maria jumped. 'There's Briggs! For God's sake go now! I'll do what I can about thy job at t' mill, I promise.'

The door closed quickly and Jess heard

237

Maria running back and calling out with feigned gaiety to Briggs. Poor Maria. For all her wilfulness she had made a hard bed for herself to lie upon.

It was as Jess was climbing the long hill towards home that he heard the clop-clop of hoofbeats ahead of him. He raised his eyes from moodily surveying the track beneath his feet, and saw a portly figure on horseback approaching him. Deferentially Jess moved off the track on to the heather to allow him to pass, but the figure slowed as he neared him. Jess started guiltily when he recognised Justice Radcliffe. The magistrate reined in his horse and greeted Jess cheerily.

'It's Drake, isn't it, from Denshaw's? I heard you were ill and am glad to see you're recovered.'

Jess nodded his thanks, but could not bring himself to speak. A pebble seemed to be lodged in his throat, so large and constricting a lump could he feel there. Radcliffe rubbed his chin. 'Let me see, you were ill at the time of this sad business when my friend Denshaw was so cruelly murdered, I remember. I was not able to ask you in for questioning with the others.'

The lurch in Jess's heart shifted the pebble. He opened his mouth to speak, but he did not know what to say. Radcliffe spoke first. 'But as I remember now, Miss Denshaw told me you were sent home ill from the mill some time before her father was attacked. So you would be abed and unaware of what happened, I take it.' Jess stood silent. 'You've no doubt heard of the reward my fellow magistrates have offered?'

Jess looked desperately at the horse's hooves, as if the answer to his dilemma could be found there. His oath, his sacred vow not to speak! And he had repeated his promise to Mellors the night before!

Radcliffe was regarding him fixedly. 'I know of your good repute, Drake. I feel if there were aught you had come to hear of this matter, you would do all you could to bring these foul blackguards to justice. Is that not so?'

Jess had no choice but to speak now. He cleared his throat and stammered, fearing that his reddening face would give him away. 'I – I – should indeed like to see Mr Denshaw avenged, sir, and his m – murderers punished,' he stuttered, 'but I fear there is naught I can tell thee to help thee.'

That much was true anyway, in the face of his promise to Mellors, but it was difficult not to speak an outright lie. Radcliffe watched him, nodding his grey head thoughtfully.

'He'll be avenged, Drake, have no fear on that score. I shall not rest until I track the wretches down. But even if I fail, they will not escape.'

He smiled to see Jess's face, puzzled at this enigmatic statement. 'You're a God-fearing man, are you not, Drake?'

'Aye sir.'

'Well, remember the words "Vengeance is mine; I will repay, saith the Lord."? I believe them to be true. Even if I fail to catch and punish those who are lurking in the shadows, full of guilt at what they have done, the Lord will find a way to punish them for their crime. To the end of their days they will go on paying for their misdeeds.'

Jess listened to him open-mouthed. The magistrate dug his heels into the horse's flanks and rode off, with a cheery, 'Good day to you, Drake.'

His heart filled with misgivings, Jess trudged on. Did Radcliffe perhaps suspect that Jess knew more than he was willing to tell, and was he possibly warning Jess that even if no one discovered his secret he would still be punished?

It was no comfort to Jess that his was not the hand that had pulled the trigger. To have witnessed a murder and held his tongue was tantamount to being an accomplice in the conspiracy. But on the other hand he had to weigh in the balance his vow of silence to Mellors. Lord, how difficult life was!

He turned over Radcliffe's words in his mind as he returned up the lane towards his cottage. God would punish the evil-doers, he had said, exacting His vengeance in His own way. The unpleasant thought crossed Jess's weary mind that maybe he was being made to pay by losing Maggie. And come to think of it, by losing Maria's support and losing track of Jenny too.

Oh no! It was unbearable to think so! His own weakness the cause of Maggie's death? His guilty silence the reason for Jenny's disappearance? No, no! The God Jess had come to know and love in the days of chapel-going had been a God full of love and humanity, not a revenge-seeking master determined to punish an erring servant.

But Radcliffe was an educated man, perhaps better versed in the ways of God than himself after all his years of book-learning. Could it be that he was right, and Jess would suffer now till the end of his days for his wrongdoing? Already he had lost Maggie, Maria and, it seemed, Jenny too.

He could not hasten his steps towards the little cottage fast enough. Abigail and Seth were there alone and had been for several hours. He was anxious to reassure himself that all was well with them.

But when he flung open the door and looked about him, there was no one there.

'Abigail! Abigail! Where art tha?' he cried, panic rising inside him. No answer came to his frantic call. He rushed through the cottage to the bedroom, but only Maggie's body lay there under the blanket. He rushed up to the upper room, hoping to find Abigail asleep on her little bed with the babe in her arms, but empty beds and the dusty, silent loom were all that met his anxious eyes.

'Abigail!' His voice rose and sank in a cry of infinite pathos. Dear God, let him not have lost her and the baby too! A woman's voice called up the stairs.

'Jess Drake? It's Mrs Benson here!'

Jess nearly fell headlong down the stairs in his anxiety to reach her. 'Have you seen Abigail?' he cried, clutching the woman's shoulders.

'Don't take on so, Jess,' Mrs Benson said reproachfully, gently loosening his fingers. 'She's safe and well, down at my house.'

'Thank God, thank God,' Jess moaned, his knees feeling suddenly weak and trembling.

'She had t' good sense to come to me wi'

t' babby, not knowing how to cope wi' him herself. She told me about Maggie. I came up earlier and laid her out for thee. T' best nightdress I could find.'

Jess was too relieved at hearing Abigail and Seth were safe to register what the woman was saying. He understood vaguely that he was in her debt, but somehow the words of gratitude did not come.

'I'll send Abigail home now tha'rt back, but I'd best keep Seth a bit. He's poorly and needs nursing. I tried to give him a bit o' rag dipped i' broth for him to suck, but he couldn't keep it down, poor lamb.'

Jess was not listening to her. He was luxuriating in the warming thought that Radcliffe was wrong. Abigail, the jewel of his heart, was alive and well. Together they'd manage, Abbie and he, to see to Seth till Jenny came home. For the first time in days optimism began to glow feebly in his heart.

Eighteen

Afterwards, Jess could barely remember the events of that week clearly. It passed in a buzz of activity, on Mrs Benson's part rather than on his. She tended little Seth and organised a collection amongst the neighbouring valley folk to raise enough money for Maggie's funeral.

'A copper here and there and it soon mounts up,' she said proudly as she handed over the money to Jess. 'We couldn't have poor Maggie put in a pauper's grave, not after t' hardworking life she led.'

It was true, thought Jess. Maggie had been the finest wife and mother any man could ask for. If only she had died believing in him! He tried to thank Mrs Benson, but she would not listen. She brushed aside his gratitude with an impatient wave.

'By the way,' she added, turning in the doorway, 'I've enough left to pay old Isaiah to come and be t' sin-eater, so all's taken care of.'

She was taken aback by the suddenness with which Jess leapt to his feet. 'Nay, nay, no sin-eater,' he cried, a choke in his voice.

'Whyever not, pray? It's been t' tradition for many a long year hereabouts. Old Isaiah earns his living by it, and it'd be a shame to lay Maggie in her grave wi' her sins still upon her.'

'No sin-eater for my Maggie,' Jess said sharply, and there was no arguing with the finality of his tone. It sickened Jess to think of old Isaiah, ninety if he was a day, standing by Maggie's grave, munching toothlessly on the oatcake and sipping the water to signify his absorption of poor Maggie's sins. He knew he would feel an irresistible urge to dash the cup from the old man's lips. What sins had Maggie ever committed in all her life that needed atonement? It was he, Jess, who was permeated with guilt and sinfulness! It was he whom the old man should be trying to cleanse, not poor, innocent Maggie!

The day they laid Maggie to rest in the earth was a bright, golden day of early summer. It seemed all wrong to Jess that the sun should have the temerity to shine on a tragic scene like this, and the mills to clatter on, regardless of her passing. Few mourners stood by the graveside, for most folk who had not lost their jobs were at their work. Maria, he was sad to see, did not appear. Nor Jenny. Wherever she had gone, she could not have heard of her mother's death, or she would undoubtedly have come.

Jess stood bareheaded, feeling the warmth of the sun on the nape of his neck as they lowered Maggie's small coffin out of sight. Abigail clung to his wrist and watched silently. She shed no tears, either too benumbed with shock, or stunned by the rapidity of change in her young life. Mrs Benson nodded and hurried away as soon as the brief ceremony was over, to get back to baby Seth.

But despite all her determined efforts, the baby followed its mother into the grave within the week. Jess's heart was now too wracked with grief and guilt to feel any more pain. To think that only four months ago he had been so overjoyed and proud at the birth of his son, and yet he could find no grief in his heart at his premature death. It was the measure of Jess's profound and utter despair, that he could feel no more.

Day succeeded day, long and hot and empty. Abigail went dutifully to the mill at sunrise and came home at sunset, red-eyed and exhausted and usually crept into her bed, too tired to eat. Jess sat dull-eyed by the empty grate and barely noticed her, engulfed in grief and self-pity.

Indecision still wracked him. He was convinced now that Radcliffe was right and a curse lay upon him and his family. Was it too late to avert further misfortune by confessing to the authorities what he knew of Denshaw's murder? Confession, however, would mean having to reveal that he had been a Ludd himself, involved in machine-breaking, and he could not bear to think of Abigail left alone if he were imprisoned. Moreover, there was still his promise to Mellors. Oh God, what was he to do?

In June the air of the valley seemed to change. Till then the local people, silent and withdrawn after the terrible shock that Denshaw's murder had given them, ceased to applaud the Luddites' activities and no more was to be heard of them, as if they had all disappeared underground. The valley folk had had to cope with unemployment too. Parliament's Orders in Council had left the manufacturers no outlet for their goods, and one by one the workers found themselves laid off until very few families still had a breadwinner in work.

But now Parliament was moved to action, stirred by the violence of feeling in the Colne Valley. The Orders in Council were replaced, and manufacturers took on again gladly the workers they had been forced to lay off. Jess was woken from his apathy one day by a young lad knocking at his door. 'Mester Drake? I've a message for thee from thy daughter.'

'Jenny?' Jess asked eagerly, a stir of hope in his heart. He had never been able to bring himself to believe other than that she would return home sooner or later.

The lad looked puzzled. 'Nay, Maria she said her name were. She said to tell thee as Mester Briggs wants thee at t' mill.'

So Jess, like many others, found himself back at his loom. His wage, added to Abigail's, meant that they could eat again, modestly but at least sufficiently well to be able to regain their strength. But still Abigail looked peaked and wan and vacant.

Inside the gloom of the mill, Jess was unaware, save for the heat, of the glorious summer slipping by outside its grey stone walls. He was aware, however, of the air of returning peace and satisfaction amongst his fellow workers. Smiles now lit their faces from time to time, and they greeted each other cheerfully. There was a feeling of optimism in the air, for trade was booming and work was plentiful again.

Their optimism began to filter through to

Jess's darkened heart. Life could not go on for ever being tragic and grief-laden, could it? There must be some happiness ahead for Abigail and himself, and Jenny too one day, he hoped.

The leaves had fallen from the trees in Dungeon Wood, though the days were still warm and sunny for the time of year. Jess found Mrs Benson awaiting him at his door when he returned home one evening.

'Hast heard?'

'What?'

'They arrested George Mellors and Ben Walker.'

Jess's heart lurched. 'What for?'

'Don't know. Denshaw business, I reckon.'

Jess thought it over. 'Radcliffe, was it?' If so, there was a chance his own name would be brought out, and then what?

'Aye, but he had to let 'em go again this aft, seemingly. So he can't have learnt owt.'

Jess did not know whether to feel relief or despair. It crossed his mind that it was odd Mrs Benson should relay this news to him, unless, of course, she knew his connection with Mellors.

'Thought he'd given it up, old Radcliffe, trying to find t' murderers, but it seems he's still at it,' Mrs Benson went on. 'I hope he gets 'em in t' end, whoever they are. There's

nobody cares for t' Ludds now after that do.'
She was giving him an odd, querying look.
Jess felt defensive.

'I'm no Ludd,' he stated flatly.

'Aye, well, tha's nowt to worry about, hast
tha?' She drew her shawl tightly about her
ample figure and left him. Jess prepared
supper for Abigail thoughtfully. If only
Radcliffe were to catch the miscreants
without Jess's help, and if only Mellors felt
as bound by the oath of secrecy as he did,
then he would be safe. Maybe then the
curse would lift. Maybe then vengeance
would stop punishing him and his family.

It was late October. Justice Radcliffe was
entertaining Susannah Denshaw to dinner
in Milnsbridge House.

'Another glass of claret, my dear?'

'Thank you, no. Tell me, Mr Radcliffe, do
you think it is likely that the fellows who
murdered my father will ever be caught
now, after all this time? In six months they
have had plenty of time to hide, flee the
country even.'

The magistrate looked at her quizzically.
'You still demand vengeance then, Susannah?'

'Dear me, no! Revenge is the furthest
thought from my mind! I was shocked and

grieved at Papa's death, naturally, but at the back of it all I couldn't help feeling a certain amount of sympathy for the poor fellows. Stupid and misguided fellows they must have been, but they suffered much and were hardly accountable for what they did. No, they have my pity rather than my hatred, Mr Radcliffe.'

'You are a sympathetic soul, my dear, nonetheless justice must be done if it is at all possible. I wish to blazes I could find sufficient evidence to bring the culprits to justice, for I know full well who their leader was, but can I prove it? And each day that passes makes the possibility of finding such evidence less and less likely. I am ashamed to have to confess it, my dear, but outside a providential stroke of luck, I fear I shall never be able to bring a case against the wretches. But I shall never give up the attempt. Of that you may rest assured.'

'I'm sure I can. Robert feels so too, for he said as much before he left for London.'

'How are you managing with the business, Susannah, without Robert's help?'

Susannah smiled. 'Oh, well enough. Charles is a wonderful businessman. And I do not plan to remain at Brackenhurst much longer.'

Radcliffe set down his glass sharply.

'You're not leaving us, Susannah? Grief has not driven you to forsake the Colne Valley, has it?'

Susannah blushed and dimpled. 'Indeed no. It is only that – Captain Northcliffe has proposed to me, and I have accepted. After our wedding I shall make my home at York with his parents.'

'And the mill?'

Susannah shrugged. 'Robert must decide what is to be done about that. The business is thriving now, and if he prefers to remain in London, no doubt he will appoint a manager to see to matters here for him.'

'I see. Well, allow me to wish you every happiness in your forthcoming marriage, my dear. Captain Northcliffe is indeed a charming and competent young man, and I've no doubt you'll be very happy together.'

As Susannah smiled her thanks the housekeeper ushered in Captain Northcliffe. He saluted the magistrate, explaining that he had called to escort Miss Denshaw home.

Radcliffe congratulated him on his good fortune, and then turned to other matters. 'Any movements in the valley?' he asked.

'Not a flicker, sir. Nor has there been any sign of the Ludds in all these months. I think it may not be long before the general moves the cavalry out of Huddersfield and details us to another mission. Your mills and machines are no longer in need of our defence.'

Radcliffe sighed. 'Your men have been most useful in intercepting those found lurking on the moors at night and interrogating them. If you leave, I shall have to carry on with the help of only the constables. It will be hard work. I hope the general leaves you here at least a little longer, till the murderers are caught.'

Both men looked at the floor. Susannah knew that neither of them wanted to admit, especially before her, that the task was hopeless. A knock came at the door.

'Come in!' Radcliffe barked gruffly.

The housekeeper entered. 'There's a woman to see you, sir.'

'A woman? What way is that to announce a lady, Sarah? What is her name?'

'I don't know, sir. She wouldn't give her name. But she's not a lady, sir, she's a – woman,' the housekeeper ended helplessly.

'Show her in.' There was a puzzled note in Radcliffe's voice, and Susannah shared it. She regarded the bent, ragged old woman who shambled in, wary-eyed and defensive, with unconcealed curiosity.

'Art tha Mester Radcliffe?' the old woman addressed the magistrate.

'I am.'

'I want to talk to thee.'

'Do so.'

'In private, I mean. I have summat to tell thee as might interest thee.'

'Is it concerning the death of Mr Denshaw?' It was a shot in the dark. Susannah knew by Radcliffe's tone that he was only guessing, but there was hope in his voice. And it was evident from the old woman's start of surprise that his shot found its mark.

'How didst tha know?' she stuttered in amazement.

'Never mind. Tell me what you know.'

Susannah sat forward on the edge of her chair. Was this the stroke of providence that Radcliffe had prayed for?

'There's a reward, isn't there?' the old woman countered. 'Two thousand pound, I'm told.'

'There is, if your information leads to the murderer's arrest.'

The ragged creature stared aggressively at the officer in uniform and at Susannah. 'I'd rather talk to thee alone,' she growled. 'I want to make a bargain wi' thee.'

'No.' Radcliffe's voice was stern. 'It is your duty as a citizen to reveal all you know, otherwise you are obstructing justice and that is an offence.'

The old woman's eyes widened in fear. 'Here, don't threaten me, I came to help thee.'

'Then do so.'

She fiddled with the fringe of her shawl. 'I know someone as can give thee all t' information tha wants. Only I want an assurance that no harm will come to him – and that he'll get t' reward.'

'I see. The man you refer to is himself involved in the murder I take it, and you wish to protect him.'

She nodded vigorously. 'Aye, and he'll get t' reward too, won't he?'

Radcliffe considered her thoughtfully for a moment. 'Turning King's evidence will undoubtedly earn him a recommendation to mercy, I am sure, though I cannot guarantee it for the case will have to be tried before the Assizes.'

'But tha'll speak for him, won't tha?' she demanded eagerly, 'and see he gets paid?'

'I think I can vouch for that, but first I must see if his information is what I need.'

'If tha promise his safety, I'll bring him to thee, tonight, if tha will.'

'Then go now and bring him to me. I'll take down his deposition, and then we shall know.'

The old woman turned and began hurrying away, eager to get the matter over and done with, and the promised reward guaranteed. Radcliffe called after her. 'One moment, my good woman. Your name, if you please, and that of the informer.'

The old woman's expression tightened a little at the sound of the unsavoury word. Then she drew herself up. 'My name is Mrs Walker, and the man who's to help thee is my son, Ben Walker.'

As soon as she had gone Susannah drew breath again. Radcliffe turned to her and Northcliffe and smiled, a taut, satisfied smile.

'They say money speaks,' he said slowly. 'Well, it certainly loosens tongues. I had almost given up hope. And to think I had Walker and that blackguard Mellors in this very room only two weeks ago, and both swore to being innocent as babes. I knew them to be liars, but could not prove it – till now. But tonight, if Walker speaks the truth, we'll have our case, and Mellors and the rest will be up before the next Assizes.'

Susannah rose to leave. 'I'd rather not be here,' she said quietly.

'Of course, my dear. But rest assured that now justice will be done.'

'I'll send up guards,' Captain Northcliffe

promised. 'You'll need them if you're to make arrests. I'll return immediately.'

Radcliffe nodded his thanks. He smiled as he watched Northcliffe helping Susannah with great solicitude to put on her pelisse. It had turned out to be a satisfying evening after all.

After the young couple had left he set out his pens and paper on his desk with great deliberation, then sat and tapped his fingers together impatiently as he waited. At last he heard the doorbell ring and the housekeeper admitting visitors.

'Excuse me, sir,' Sarah said, knocking and peering round the door, 'but there's that – woman again, and she's got a man with her this time. Walker, she says the name is.'

'Show them in, Sarah,' said Radcliffe contentedly.

Nineteen

Justice Radcliffe sat lingering over his breakfast a few days later, relishing more than usual the savoury ham Sarah had cooked for him. He read and re-read with immense satisfaction the same paragraph in the *Leeds Mercury*.

'A man has been taken up and examined by that indefatigable magistrate, Joseph Radcliffe, Esq., and has given the most complete and satisfactory evidence of the murder of Mr Josiah Denshaw. The villains accused have been frequently examined before but have always been discharged for want of sufficient evidence. The man charged behaved with the greatest effrontery till he saw the informer, when he changed colour and gasped for breath. When he came out of the room after hearing the informer's evidence, he exclaimed, "Damn that fellow, he had done me!" ... This will lead to many more apprehensions.'

True enough, thought Radcliffe. Walker had been only too anxious to tell all he knew in the expectation of the reward, and there wasn't a Ludd in the valley whose name Radcliffe did not know. Soon, very soon, all the ringleaders would be rounded up and dealt with as severely as the law would allow. The Luddites would never trouble this valley again. Thank God for the Judases of this world, the men easily corruptible by the promise of money. Radcliffe had reason to be pleased with himself.

The news came to the valley folk with the

unexpectedness of a thunderclap. Jess knew nothing of it until the break for drinking time in the mill.

'Hast heard, they've got Mellors and Thorpe for t' murder, and Smith and Walker too,' Ramsbottom told him, ashen-faced. 'They've been sent off i' a coach to York for t' Assizes, all but Walker, and he's been sent to Chester, they tell me.'

Jess looked at him aghast. 'Mellors, caught?'

'Aye, somebody split on 'em, seemingly. They say it were Ben Walker, and that's why he's been sent to Chester, so t' Ludds can't get at him and shut him up.'

So Walker had broken his vow of silence! Jess felt a flood of guilty relief. Walker had saved him from having to break his own oath, if ever he could have brought himself to make the decision. Ramsbottom went on to tell him that according to the newspaper more arrests were to follow, and for the next week he and Jess and many other men in the valley held their breath and waited. A penalty of death was not to be dismissed lightly. They heard how the men who worked in John Wood's cropping shop were interrogated and arrested, and then others, and then still more. A hush of expectancy lay over the valley, but the days went by and no one came to question Jess.

He was standing over his loom one day, immersed in thought, when Briggs came and tapped him on the shoulder.

'Come outside,' Briggs bawled above the clatter.

Jess followed him out into the November dankness. Briggs shifted uneasily from one foot to the other.

'Thy lass, Jenny,' he began clumsily. 'Hast tha heard aught of her of late?'

Jess started. 'Nay,' he answered slowly. 'Why dost ask?'

Briggs looked at the cobblestones at his feet. 'Tha'd best get up to t' dam. They've just fished a lass out o' t' water, seemingly, and they think she could be thy lass.'

Jess stumbled out of the mill yard and along the river bank, stunned and disbelieving. The girl was dead, whoever she was, he knew by Briggs' embarrassment. It could not be Jenny. No, never Jenny.

But as he neared the knot of men clustered round a prostrate figure lying dripping and inert on the pathway, he knew with a sudden conviction that it was Jenny. A perfunctory glance at the matted, slime-green hair that had once been fair, and the bloated grey face was enough. He turned away with revulsion and sank down on his knees, overcome with nausea.

They picked him up and helped him back to the mill.

'Get back to thy loom,' snapped Briggs with a harshness that Jess knew he was using deliberately to avoid any suggestion of sympathy. 'There's orders to be met, and work can't wait on thee all day.'

In a way Jess was glad of the monotony of the relentless machine demanding his attention, depriving him of the opportunity to think. Briggs flailed right and left with his whip, attacking the small children with vicious abandon, as though to persuade Jess that there was no room for sentimentality in the mill.

Poor Jenny, he mused. How had she come to end thus, he wondered sadly. It must have been an accident, for surely she would never have drowned herself deliberately, not Jenny. And where had she been all these months? If she had been so close all this time, he must have come to hear of it. She must have gone away and was on her way home to him when the accident happened. On her way home, he was sure of it. He'd always believed she would return.

The sad news he broke to Abigail that evening seemed to wash over her like waves over a rock, receding and leaving no trace of their passage. She simply stared at him uncomprehendingly and went on spooning her food listlessly into her mouth. It seemed as if she too had borne all the suffering her small frame was capable of feeling, and she had no capacity left to feel any more.

Jess was sorrowful, not only at this latest tragic blow to strike his family, but also to see what devastation such suffering could cause. Abigail and himself, he thought, were no more than pale spectres of themselves, walking and eating, sleeping and working like other folk, but devoid of any emotion.

Jenny went, unwept, into her grave alongside her mother and baby brother. On Christmas Day Mrs Benson tried to cheer their day by bringing them a generous helping of the chicken she had killed and cooked specially for the occasion. Jess too made an effort to give the day a festive air by taking Abigail to chapel for once, but the child simply sat there dispassionately, as if unaware of the happy folk in their Sunday best, carolling their gladness that life was beginning anew.

After their one day holiday Jess and Abigail returned to work. Christmas soon faded into a memory, and with the new year snow came to the valley. Jess heard that the York Assizes were now in session, and

Mellors, Thorpe and the others were on trial for their lives. He could hardly feel enough to rejoice that he was not one of the sixty-four Luddites taken and lying in York Castle, more than half of them on capital charges.

He heard all the events at York quickly enough, either from his fellow workers at the mill who had learned to read and were able to retell the reports in the *Mercury*, or from those who pestered the local school-master daily for information.

'Two judges and three counsel to defend Mellors and t' others,' Ramsbottom told him as they stood together at the mill gate the day the trial began. He stamped his feet and blew clouds of hazy breath into the cold air, and flung his thin arms back and forth across his chest to warm himself. 'But I think even them three'll be hard put to it to get them off. I hear as there's two other informers as well as Ben Walker, so their evidence'll be enough to hang 'em all.'

And so it transpired. After listening for ten hours to damning evidence given by Walker, and Hall and Sowden, two of the men from John Wood's cropping shop, the jury took only twenty-five minutes to return a verdict of guilty on Mellors, Thorpe and Smith. The condemned men remained silent to the end, making no confession of their guilt, and two days after their sentences they were hanged in York.

Jess could find no words when he was told, nor feeling in his heart except deep gloom. This was only the beginning of the York Assizes. By the time it was concluded, many more Luddites, over a hundred in all, had been arrested and tried. Ben Walker's greed and loose tongue had begun a long trail. Some of these unfortunates, many misled rather than wilfully malicious, were hanged, others transported or imprisoned. Jess felt a pang of guilt penetrate his apathy when he heard of those punished for the Rawfolds mill attack. By rights he too should have been on trial among them. It was something of a reassurance to him, however, that once the ringleaders were disposed of, the judges discharged many on bail, on condition that they lived henceforth honestly and industriously.

Jess hung his head in shame. He too must atone for his involvement with this lawlessness. He too must live honestly and industriously for the rest of his days. Had he not paid forfeit enough for his misdeeds, losing most of his beloved family one by one?

Thus he reasoned and argued with himself. The Assizes were over, work went on in the valley as usual, and life began to settle down to normality again. William Hall returned on the coach from York, and the whole valley turned its back on him for his treachery.

'They'd a got Mellors in any case, wi' Walker's evidence, but they'd nowt to prove who were in t' Rawfolds business till Hall bleated to save hisself,' Ramsbottom growled angrily. 'How he has t' face to show hissen here again I'll never know. But he'll not be able to stand it, if I know owt. He'll be bound to leave again ere long.'

Ramsbottom's prophetic words were echoed in the case of Ben Walker too. He hastened back to Huddersfield, freed for his co-operation as Radcliffe had promised, and rushed to Milnsbridge House to claim his reward. His dreams of life in comfort with all the luxuries of a gentleman's existence were short-lived. The huge reward he confidently expected had not, after all, been offered by the crown as he believed, but by a committee set up to prosecute the Luddites. Walker applied for his reward but the committee, content now they had achieved their aims, resolutely disregarded his requests.

It was now well into the New Year 1813, and the valley folk resumed their lives and tried to forget, hoping that life would take on a new and kindlier shape in this New Year. The snow on the moorland slopes was beginning to melt and recede. Jess, among the others, found that the daily pattern had a soothing effect, and as time passed and he and Abigail evolved their own way of life together, he began to feel a faint but distinguishable tinge of hope.

After all, the murdered man had been avenged. The Luddite movement had virtually ceased to exist, deprived of their leaders and aware now of their own short-sighted misguidedness. And then one evening, trudging home from the mill, up the slushy moorland track, Jess met Justice Radcliffe riding down on horseback, as he had done once before.

'Evening Drake,' the portly magistrate greeted him cheerily. 'All well with you, I hope?'

'Thankee sir, and wi' thee?'

'Going to watch the wedding on Saturday?'

'Whose wedding, sir?'

'Why, Miss Denshaw and Captain Northcliffe. I thought all the valley would be at the parish church to see that. Glad day for Miss Susannah, after all she's been through lately.'

'Aye, sir.'

'Bad business, but the score is settled now. I reckon we disposed of the real culprits. I'm well aware there were others in the Luddite movement who never came to trial,' Radcliffe said, and Jess wondered whether he was imagining the pointed look the magistrate gave him. 'But they've naught to fear now. Vengeance has been exacted.'

As he rode on up the hill Jess remembered Radcliffe's words on their first meeting. 'Vengeance is mine; I will repay, saith the Lord.' Was he now saying that atonement was over, finished? That would confirm the opinion Jess himself was beginning to feel. The flicker of optimism began to glow more strongly.

Susannah and Captain Northcliffe were married on a frosty, sunlit day and soon afterwards the cavalry were sent away and Susannah went too. The ice-cold winds at length gave up the struggle to prolong the winter and died away. New shoots appeared above ground and on the trees of Dungeon Wood, and the air of the valley breathed new life and hope. Jess was delighted to see Abigail gradually gaining a new sparkle due, no doubt, to more frequent eating and the resurgence of spring. At length she even began to speak again.

'It's lonely wi'out me mam,' she said one day.

'I know, lovey, but we're busy, thee and me, wi' our work. We've no time for brooding,' Jess consoled her.

'And Seth and Jenny gone too,' she said sadly.

'But we've still each other, haven't we lass?'

She smiled, a faint, reluctant smile, but he knew that she loved him as deeply as he adored her. His Abigail, the sunlight of his life, would soon regain her vigour and be the joy of his old age that he'd always known she would be.

'What's it like i' thy mill?' he asked. She'd never spoken of it. She shrugged.

'Not so bad. There's only about twenty of us, all lasses, and when t' overseer's out we can talk.'

'And when he's in?'

'We dursn't speak. He's too keen wi' his billy roller and his whip. But he's out more often than not. He likes his drink, old Schofield.'

'I see. And is he t' only man in t' mill then?'

'Aye. Well, there's a lad to do t' odd jobs and fetch messages, young Billy. Usually he's kept busy being sent to fetch ale from t' public house for Schofield. Apart from him there's nobody.'

It sounded tolerable enough, as mill work went. Jess felt somewhat appeased that his precious Abbie did not have to undergo the vicious treatment constantly that Briggs meted out to the little ones in Denshaw's mill.

It came as a surprise, therefore, when Abigail said in a small voice one clear morning that she wished she did not have to go to work. Jess asked her why.

'Me legs ache summat awful, standing so long, Father. We dursn't sit for a moment, or we get beaten.'

Jess understood. Fourteen hours' standing was hard for such young legs as Abigail's. He looked at her critically. No, there was no sign of the buckled legs that so many of the Denshaw children had.

'Tha'rt tired, lovey, that's all. But tomorrow's Sunday and tha can rest i' bed all day if tha wishes. Come on, lass, let's be off or we'll be late,' he urged her.

She said nothing, and set off beside him, taking three quick little steps to match every long stride of his. Outside Denshaw's gate they parted, and he watched her trudge on down the hill before he turned into the mill yard. She was a good 'un, and no mistake.

269

Just like her mother, bless her, plenty of courage and no whining.

He was still glowing with pride and love of her when he saw Briggs blocking his way at the door.

'I've summat to tell thee, Drake,' the bigger man stated.

'Oh aye?'

'Mrs Briggs is dead. Thy Maria and me's getting wed on Saturday. Tha can come to t' wedding if tha wants.'

Jess was too taken aback at Briggs' bald statement to reply. But inwardly he was glad that Maria's position in Briggs' house was to be legalised. Now no tongues could wag about his daughter's looseness. The valley folk might be poor but they were the epitome of rectitude and propriety, and if Maria had stayed on after Mrs Briggs' death unwed, there'd have been gossip for months. It was a pity that the wedding was so soon after her death, however. Briggs seemed to read his thoughts.

'She's expecting,' he said quickly, and turned away.

Jess followed him in, pondering on this latest item of news. That explained it. Poor Maria. She'd soon have eight bairns to cope with, as well as Briggs' irascible temper.

It was late afternoon when he heard the

commotion outside Briggs' office. He looked up. A white-faced man was pouring out a
gabble of confused words and gesticulating.
Briggs pointed to Jess. The man hurried
towards him.

'Art tha Jess Drake?' he shouted. Jess
nodded.

'Fire at Atkinson's. Girls all locked in.
Can't get 'em out,' he cried.

Oh God, no! Jess cried inwardly. Abigail!

Twenty

Jess neither thought nor cared about asking
Briggs' permission. He simply left his loom,
the shuttle flying back and forth untended,
and fled. He raced out of the mill yard and
down the hill as fast as his trembling legs
would carry him, the messenger hard on his
heels.

He could smell the odour of acrid smoke
long before Atkinson's came into sight, and
see the smoke-cloud lying heavy over the
valley. The panic and terror in his heart
would not be beaten down until he knew his
beloved Abigail was safe. Oh God, dear

God, punish me no more! he cried inwardly. Leave me my Abbie, only my Abbie, I beg you!

He sped round the corner and saw the flames from the upper storey licking round the eaves. No, no, it could not be! The girls must have been released by now and be standing watching in horror from a safe distance! If not, oh God, if not, there was no justice in this world!

He rushed up to the knot of people standing gazing in fascination at the red glow, and pulled one of them frantically by the arm. 'Where art t' lasses? Are they out?' he cried.

The stranger shook his head. 'No key,' he said laconically.

'Then why isn't someone doing summat about it?' Jess shouted desperately. 'Water, for God's sake!'

'It's no use, t' mill's nearly burnt out now, can't tha see? There's only t' roof and that's nearly gone now.'

A constable was holding a young boy by the arm. Jess rushed to him. 'Axes, summat to break t' door down, quick!'

'They've been sent for, but I reckon it's too late. There'll be nobody left after that blaze. Now come on, Billy,' the constable said to the lad.

The boy wriggled in his grip. His eyes,

272

reddened with smoke, were wide in terror. Jess watched, stupefied. 'I know nowt no more, honest,' the boy whined. 'Mester Schofield sent me down into t' store room to chase t' rats out, that's all.'

'How couldst tha see 'em down in t' dark?'

'Mester Schofield gave me a candle.'

'A candle? Wi' all that raw cotton there?'

'Aye, I know, but how else could I see 'em?'

'And what happened?'

The boy wriggled in the constable's firm grip again. 'I don't rightly know. A big rat, bigger'n my arm it were, jumped at me. I think I dropped t' candle.'

The constable looked at him in silence for a moment. 'And where were Mester Schofield all this time.'

'How should I know? Once he's got his ale he goes off somewhere. He locked t' lasses in so's none of 'em could get out, and then he went. It's a wonder he's not back.'

The constable let go of the boy's shoulder and he shot off into the crowd. The constable then turned to Jess, who was standing listening in stunned silence.

'Is one o' them lasses your'n?'

'Aye, aye – did any of 'em get out?' Jess demanded eagerly.

A blacksmith, still wearing his leather

apron and sweating from his forge, cut between Jess and the constable. 'Stand back,' he commanded.

It took the burly blacksmith several minutes with his enormous sledgehammer to break down the door. Jess watched, hypnotised. It was Enoch, the Luddites' sledgehammer, he could swear, and it was the night of Rawfolds all over again. Rawfolds – and Booth – and his severed leg.

It was like watching a horrifying, silent re-enactment of that night, but this time it was played to a hushed, motionless audience. No Luddite cries, no bullets whining this time, only the crashing of Enoch on the door. Finally the door splintered and fell.

Jess was still in a state of trance as men began to fight their way in through the smoke. He jerked himself awake and pushed his way into the darkened, smoke-logged interior after them.

'Abigail! Abigail!' he called, but the words choked in his throat as the smoke entered and suffocated his lungs. He fought on, coughing and with his eyes streaming. Men stooped and knelt before him. Jess fell on his knees and crawled towards them. They were picking up charred pieces of timber, and Jess was puzzled.

The fight to gain air for his lungs drove

him finally outside again. People were bending over the charred fragments and weeping unashamedly. The constable took Jess's arm.

'It's no good, lad, I told thee. None of 'em got out. This is all that remains of 'em.' He pointed to the fragments. Jess's gaze followed his finger.

'This? Tha means – the lasses?'

'Aye, lad. Tha should a seen the fury o' that fire. Nowt'd survive that. There'll be no bodies to bury, I'm thinking, just these.'

No, it was too revolting to believe! Jess clung to his one last thread of hope. 'Did – didn't any of 'em get out? Not one?'

The constable eyed him sympathetically, but he could not satisfy the pathetic appeal in Jess's voice. 'I'm sorry, lad, truly sorry. That overseer'll have summat to answer for, when we find him.'

A man approached. 'We found Schofield, constable. He were sleeping it off in t' midden down there.'

'Had he the key?'

'Aye, in his pocket. Not fifty yards away.'

Jess choked at the words. Salvation for his Abbie lay so near all the time, and yet God had seen fit to take her, and the others. His anguish robbed him of the power to think or to reason. He blundered blindly away from the mill, the tears streaming down his cheeks and great sobs wracking his chest.

How long he lay in the shadow of Dungeon Wood and gave vent to his grief, Jess could not tell. But this time it was not pure, unalloyed grief he felt, but anger and bitterness too. He pummelled the grass with his hands and kicked with unquenchable rage at the tree trunks, watching the bark fly, but there was no satisfaction in venting his anger so.

God had cheated him. Just as life was beginning anew for Abbie and himself it had seemed that God's anger was appeased, He saw fit to strike Jess down once more, and this time He took the last of all Jess held dear. How could He be so unjust, so cruel and uncaring?

I believed in You, if nothing else, Jess wept bitterly, and even You forsook me. You could have left me Abbie, but You took even her from me, knowing she was what I treasured most in the world. And what a cruel way for a child to die!

Jess ran through the wood, sobbing and stumbling, flinging his arms about the tree trunks and cursing God for His injustice. It was dark before his weary steps led him home. But there was no sleep or rest for Jess that night.

A few days later he stood numb and silent, at the graveside as they lowered into a communal grave the assortment of charred fragments that had once been seventeen girls. Men and women clung to each other and sobbed for their daughters, the youngest only nine years of age like Abigail, and the eldest barely eighteen. Only Jess stood silent, too bereft of emotion to feel more than dull anger and a vast, aching void of desolation.

As he walked slowly away through the churchyard he heard the subdued comments of the sightseers, fascinated by the horror of the catastrophe, who had come to watch.

'Poor devils,' one woman muttered. 'That overseer should be hanged for murder. If it were one o' mine killed, I'd tear his drunken eyes out, that I would.'

'There'll be an investigation,' someone assured her.

'Fat lot of use that'll be,' she replied scornfully. 'Who in Parliament or anywhere else cares a fig for what happens to t' likes of us, or for what goes on in t' mills either so long as they get their brass?'

She was right, thought Jess, there was no one who cared a jot for any of them. Not even God himself cared anymore. Near the church gate two men were deep in conversation.

'Oh aye,' said one. 'He kept on trying and trying, but they wouldn't pay him up. Nobody'll have owt to do wi' him now, so I hear as he's off to London soon.'

'Good luck to him, say I! There's not a soul in t' valley as wants owt to do wi' Ben Walker these days, not after what he did. But I'm glad to hear as he didn't get his reward. Serves him right, the traitor.'

So even Ben Walker had not profited after all. He too had discovered that there was no justice in this world. Bitter and frustrated, shunned by the valley folk and aware of their scorn, he was having to flee to London, penniless and an outcast. Jess could feel no pity for him. Everyone would discover, sooner or later, that just as the world was a treacherous place, so was God inhuman and unjust.

That evening Jess sat slumped in the chair by the fireside. This was the chair Maggie used to sit in and stare into the fire before she died. She had said at the end that there was nothing left to live for, and he had tried in his ignorance to persuade her that matters could only improve, and to hang on to life and keep trying.

But she had known better. She knew life

was bitter and unrewarding, and had given up the futile struggle. Dear Maggie! He had loved her so much and brought her only worry and toil.

It was almost unbelievable that only a year ago, when his son was born, Jess had been so imbued with hope and optimism for the future. God, why did You delude me so? In twelve short months You betrayed me, robbing me of wife, son and daughters, even the youngest and most precious whom I believed You were forgiving enough to spare me for my old age!

Old age! It was not far away now. At forty one had not many years left in the mills. There would be no one to care for him or shed a tear at his passing now. No one for him to care for and work for. Life was pointless, a vast, empty desert of loneliness.

And when he was gone, there would be no more Drakes in the valley, as there had been for countless generations past. A few words of pity muttered in the Warreners over a pint, and then he and all the Drake family would fade quickly into a memory, soon erased.

His sister, far away in Lancashire, would no doubt urge him with her usual practical nature to remarry, but where was the use, even if the idea did not nauseate him? The treasured memories of Maggie and Seth and Jenny and Abigail would survive only in his mind, soon to be curtailed.

Jess was hopeless, defeated. What was the use of anything any more? Life was over. There was nothing at all left to live for. Even Mellors, who had given him a momentary goal, was no more than rotting flesh and dust under the soil of York now. Like Maggie, and Seth, and Jenny, and Abigail.

Jess felt his heart break. The only thing left now was to join them, his beloved, precious family who had given point and meaning to his life. He must put an end to all this pointless existence.

He stared fixedly at the cupboard in the corner. In there, he knew, was a stout, long rope, a relic of the days when he used to load his own cloth on his donkey's back and set off down the market. It was a sturdy rope. He could take it down to Dungeon Wood, the silent possessor of all his secrets, and hide his shame and misery there just as he had done so often in the past. His old tree would not protest. Its broad branches would bear the weight of the rope and of his falling body without a murmur.

He rose and crossed slowly to the cupboard. He lifted out the rope and stood caressing its rough surface. A knock at the cottage door made him start guiltily, and he set the coil of rope down on the dresser.

'Who is it?' he called gruffly. He wanted no well-meaning Mrs Benson fussing over him now.

'Mester Drake?' a woman's voice called.

'Aye.'

'Let me in please.'

Jess crossed and opened the door reluctantly. A young woman with a shawl drawn tight about her dark hair stood expectantly on the threshold.

'What dosta want?'

She smiled nervously. 'Can I come in? It's a rather – delicate matter I've come about.'

Jess stood aside and let her enter. She stood on the hearth and seemed to deliberate how to choose her words. She was a comely young woman, and no mistake, her hair gleaming in the firelight. She had a kind of country-fresh air about her, health and vitality shining in her face.

'Well?' Jess prompted.

'It's taken me a time to find thee, Mester Drake, and I'm still not sure as tha'rt t' man I'm after.'

Jess was confused. What was the woman blethering about? He had more pressing matters on his mind than to listen to gossip, and he wished she would hurry up and get

281

it over with.

Her dark eyes were watching him closely. 'Didst have a lass working up at t' House?' she asked at length.

'Brackenhurst, dosta mean, Denshaw's house?'

'Aye, that's it.'

'I did. Our Jenny. But she's dead now.'

'Oh, I'm right sorry to hear that.' The woman's face fell momentarily, but then she went on. 'Was she a pretty lass, wi' long fair hair and a cough?'

'Aye, a shocking cough it were. Since she were in t' mill. But why dost ask about her?'

'Then I'm sure I've got t' right man. Tha knows she left t' house – Brackenhurst, I mean?'

'Aye.' Understanding was beginning to glimmer in Jess's mind. 'Tha knows where she went, is that it? Tha's come to tell me.' He could not bring himself to tell the woman in her kindness that it no longer mattered. Nothing mattered any more.

'Well, I don't know all o' t' tale. I do know as she ended up staying wi' me.'

'Where?'

'T' other side o' Halifax.'

'Tha took her in?'

'Had to. Me and my husband found her half dead on t' doorstep, sick and fainting

282

wi' cold and hunger.'

A wail pierced the air. Jess started in alarm. A baby's cry! He watched in amazement as the woman opened her shawl and began soothing and rocking a child cradled against her bosom.

'There, there, my pretty. Tha'll have thy milk afore long, my lovey, don't cry,' she murmured. She looked at Jess and smiled. 'Thy lass were near her time when we found her. She dropped this little one soon after.'

Jess was speechless. Jenny's child, was the woman saying? It was impossible! Jenny was so unlike Maria – she would never have conceived a child out of wedlock, not Jenny! Not unless, that is ... He gazed at the young woman stupefied.

'It's true, Mester Drake,' the woman said softly. 'She told us in t' end about t' young master o' t' house and what he did to her. She begged us to care for t' babby for her until she could earn enough to come back for it, but she never did. That's why I came searching. I hadn't heard she were dead.'

Jess came closer to her and bent to look at the child. The blonde hair curling in tendrils round its brow and the wide blue eyes were undoubtedly Jenny's. And in the firm set of the chin and the flaring nostrils he could see all too clearly the mark of the

Denshaw family.

So it was true. It was Jenny's child! And Robert Denshaw's too, unfortunately. Jess felt a sinking feeling. He could not let this child be taken from him too. The Denshaws would not have it! But then, he reasoned, this child, born out of wedlock, bore its mother's name – it was a Drake. A sudden flood of exultation filled his veins. There would be a Drake after all in the valley! The Denshaws could not claim the child, even if they knew of it or cared to. Then a new and wonderful thought struck him – he had a grandchild!

He turned to the young woman. 'I'm deeply grateful to thee for coming. And for taking care o' t' babby all this time. I'll see tha's paid,' he said gruffly.

The young woman shook her head and smiled. 'Nay, it's been a great pleasure for me. We've been married eight years, my Jack and me, dost see, but we've never had no childer. It were a boon and a blessing to me when thy Jenny left me her little lass to care for.' She smiled tenderly at the child in her arms. 'It'd be a blow to me to part wi' her, and that's the truth, so I'm asking thee, Mester Drake – can I keep her a while longer, till she's older? Tha'd be doing me a favour.'

Jess's heart was singing. A granddaughter, a fair, bonny lass the image of Jenny and Abigail to work and strive for, to give meaning to his life again and comfort to his age! Oh God, forgive me!

'Take her, lass, and welcome,' he said, 'And God bless thee.' He was rewarded by the joyful light in the young woman's eyes. Tears rolled down his cheeks, but this time for joy, as he accompanied the woman to the door.

She turned in the doorway and smiled up at him shyly. 'My Jack's waiting for me down at t' public house. He'll be right glad at t' news. Thy little lass'll be well cared for, I promise thee. They do say, tha knows,' she added softly, 'as childless women have oft been known to fall after nursing somebody else's child, so I can but hope.'

The moonlight fell on her upturned face, giving it an extra radiance. Jess brushed away the silly thought that she was like an angel sent from heaven on a divine message. Having noted her name and where she lived, he bade her good evening and watched her go.

'Eh – I forgot to ask thee,' he called after her. 'Didst give t' babby a name then?'

The gentle voice came back out of the darkness. 'She were t' child of a servant girl, that's all we knew, an Abigail. And as she were a lass, we called her Abigail.'

Abigail! As soon as the woman had gone Jess fell on his knees and implored forgiveness of his God. He could not voice his thanks in words and swore instead to act out his gratitude for the rest of his days, in working and providing for this child of his blood, a miraculously-restored Abigail. No matter that life in the valley was hard, and many years would pass before poverty and hardship were alleviated; he would struggle to see that this child had all that he had intended his beloved family to have, and had failed through his weakness to provide.

Abigail. He could scarcely believe it. Abigail had died and been reborn as a tiny child to give him another chance. God in His mercy was good to him.

Jess closed the shutters and lit a candle. Its gentle glow gave him sufficient light to set about putting the little house to rights. He began by throwing the coil of rope back into the cupboard.